CW00470910

The Last Gift

Michelle Mackenzie

Published by Reflective Line Publishing, 2022.

THE LAST GIFT

First edition. August 5, 2022.

Written by Michelle Mackenzie.

To my family, I love you all so much. Without you, I'd be much like the characters in this book. Stuck in a cold dark place, with no way out.

Chapter 1

The angry-sounding alarm blared into her ears. Adelia jolted awake with a scream, falling out of bed as she crashed to the floor with a thud.

She groaned, grabbing her clothes. She gritted her teeth against the cold air, shivering. This wasn't the start of her week that she was hoping for. And with the boiler being on the blink, there was only one thing that had a chance in hell of warming her bones. Coffee, and lots of it. She glanced at the time on her watch, preparing for her usual marathon to get to work on time. Half-past eight. "Shit!" she muttered to herself. Once again, she had forgotten to change the time on her alarm, leaving her with only five minutes to leave the house. Her boss and colleagues didn't like her as it was, and running late would only encourage them further. She made herself a pot of coffee, poured it into her favourite travel mug that she had bought herself for Christmas, grabbed her keys from the hallway shelf, her shoes from the door, and rushed out of the house. Inside the car, she started the ignition, driving barefoot to the Loan Industries where she worked. It wasn't until she stopped in the parking lot, did she slip on her shoes and fastened her hair into a messy bun. Looking somewhat tidier than she did when she left the house, she smoothed down her skirt-suit and carried her still-hot travel mug into the building.

She checked the time on her watch. Nine-thirty. She let out a sigh of relief as she strode up to the stairwell. The doors creaked behind her, slamming open. She smirked, for once she had arrived before the rest of the team. With her colleagues catching up, she turned and climbed the stairs. With what sounded like a herd of elephants stamping up

1

the hallway steps, she finally made it to the top floor. She gasped for breath, her heart pounding. Just as she took a step towards the office door, her colleagues barged past her, knocking Adelia to the ground. She dropped her travel mug, spilling the coffee over the floor and herself. She cried out, only to find herself alone. Not one person stopped to check on her to see if she was ok. She sucked in a breath and climbed to her feet. She dusted herself down, groaning at the coffee on her outfit. "Of course," she muttered. She checked the time again. Nine thirty-five. "Great," she said with a grumble. "Great, great, great!"

In the far corner, she noticed a woman scrubbing the dirty floor on her hands and knees. Her brown hair tangled and her clothes were dirty and scuffed from where the gravelly floor had torn at the fabric of her trousers.

"Hey, what's your name?"

"Lilian," she whispered. "I am sorry, am I in the way...? I'll—I'll move."

"In my way? Don't be ridiculous. Come on, get off the floor. It's filthy."

"Yes, I'm the one that cleans them all," Lilian replied sadly.

"Yikes. I hope you get paid well for it."

"Oh, I don't know. I get paid, though I wouldn't say it was a great payment."

"How much?" Adelia asked, now intrigued.

Lilian leaned in, whispering numbers into her ear.

"That is slavery. I will have words with the CEO, and I am sure we can sort something more suitable. Scrubbing floors, such a waste."

"Late again, Adel," a voice snapped.

Adelia rolled her eyes. "Of course, I am fully aware of the time. If you all had not pushed right past me every morning; I would be here on time. So yes, I'm the last one." She closed her eyes, suddenly remembering who she was speaking to. "Sir," she finished. She turned around to face her red-faced boss.

"Then perhaps, you should arrive a little sooner," he said without an apology.

"That's a great idea. I'll take the pay rise to go with that earlier start," she cheered, faking a smile.

"Pay rise?" he repeated, coughing violently. "I didn't offer one."

"No? I don't work for free, Sir. If I am doing longer work hours, I'll need to be paid for the extra time. Or perhaps, everyone could just stop barging into me every damn morning, as though I don't exist."

"Alright, fine. I will make a note to everyone, to watch where they are going in the future."

"Thank you, Mr Handler. I would appreciate that."

She sat at her desk and looked around at her colleagues, their glaring faces looking back at her. "I know you can all see me!"

They went back to facing their computers, grumbling to themselves. Adelia sat in her chair and switched on her computer. "Treating me like I don't exist," she muttered. "They see me fast enough when they need something."

After a long morning, she went out into the garden and pulled out her bag and unzipped it. She peered in, pulling out the lunch she had packed the night before. A sandwich, a bottle of iced mocha, a packet of crisps, and an apple. She took out her sandwich and her drink and kept the rest in her bag. She ate under a tree; sitting alone. She took a deep breath and exhaled, wondering if working for another five years was a mistake.

As soon as it was three-thirty five, she left the office and walked out. She glanced back as she got to her car, vaguely aware of her colleagues stood back, watching her. She sighed, feeling more alone than ever.

She drove away and headed home; looking forward to the spaghetti and meatballs she was going to have for dinner.

It was four thirty when she finally got home. She walked through the door and switched on the hallway light. A small animal walked towards her, greeting her at the door with a soft purr.

"Hey, Kitty. At least you're happy to see me," she said with a small smile. "Those people at work are assholes."

The next morning, she woke up early and headed to her kitchen. She poured her coffee into a flask and got ready to leave. Twenty minutes later, she was out of the door and heading to her car. She sighed, hoping that a couple of minutes earlier would stop her from being stampeded by her colleagues.

As she arrived, she pulled up to her usual spot with a frown. The parking area was unusually busy. Shrugging it off, she secured the car and made her way towards the building. She smiled, pleased that she wasn't being barged to the back of the property. "No more complaints about being the last one there."

Just as the timer on her watch chimed, she walked into the office. She stopped, gaping at the office.

"Last one, again." a voice hissed.

She closed her eyes, instantly recognising the sound of her boss' voice. "That's because I am on time, and everyone is unusually early. When did you all get here?" she demanded.

"About half an hour ago," he replied, smirking.

"That's cool. Are they getting a pay rise, or are they working the extra hours for free?"

"It's only half an hour," he laughed.

"Yes, half an hour a day. So, at the end of the week, that'd be an extra three and a half hours. Are you telling me they agreed on almost four extra hours with no pay?"

The colleagues turned to face them, looking puzzled. "Wait, what? We aren't working for free. That's bullshit!"

Her boss cleared his throat nervously. "You know, you're right. You shouldn't be working in these conditions if you aren't happy. I'll email. I am sure we can get these resolved."

"Resolved? I hope so," she scowled. "I still have another four years on my contract."

Chapter 2

Within minutes of her leaving her boss' office. Mr Handler was holding the phone receiver to his ears. She could see him frowning through the glass as he waited. Not giving it much thought, she turned away and headed to her desk, where the computer was waiting. She logged in, then opened her mocha carton so that she could drink her coffee whilst she worked.

Her shift ended as soon as the clock chimed three thirty.

Adelia walked out of the building into the employee parking lot. The gravelled surface crunched under her brown suede boots as she walked hastily towards her car.

She looked back, realising that she was alone. She knew they were avoiding her, and she didn't care. These days, she preferred to be in solitude. At least she wasn't being trampled. Adelia sighed with a heavy sense of defeat.

As she arrived home, she opened the front door, fumbling with her keys. She stepped inside the hallway, placing her keys on the shelf by the door before she strode towards the kitchen, her footsteps echoing across the laminate flooring. Then she switched on the kettle and prepared her coffee. She barely had time to pour the hot water into the waiting mug before her phone rang. Irritably, she answered the call and placed the phone on her ear and held it in place with her shoulder.

"Hello?" she greeted.

"Adelia, I've been thinking about your recent complaints about how you were being treated. I also spoke to everyone involved. Which is why I'm calling to make you an offer. I would advise you to accept it," Mr Handler stated, not bothering to announce himself.

So much for manners. "Well, I will certainly be open-minded. What is it?"

"It's a transfer to another region, but within the same company. You are our best asset, after all. But I think you'll be more than sufficient for your experience to train the new recruits. And with a record like yours, who could train them better than you?"

"Another part? Which one?" She wondered if the other region was close by, although she hadn't heard of another district in the city. Still, she could be wrong. Doubtful, but it wasn't unheard of.

"It is rather far, but I am sure things would be more pleasant for you."

She fell silent as she considered what he was saying. "Alright, but where is it?"

"Good answer. It's in the next state. It's not too much of a distance, but it might mean you'll have to use a boat to get there. Just across the water.

"Across the water?" she repeated, just to be sure she heard correctly. "The Hampshire State. I didn't know there was one." The Hampshire State? I had not expected to be sent so far. I would prefer to stay in Cylion City."

"That isn't what I am offering you. The one in Hampshire State is the next one closest to here. It has been open for six months. You know the company well enough. Plus, you would do the same job, dealing with files and data- but you would also manage a team there. You will make sure it's running how the rest of the companies are. I am assuming you handle it?"

"Managing the company, wouldn't that be a promotion and a pay rise?"

Mr Handler muttered under his breath, forcing the words out. "Yes, a pay rise and your own office."

"That's great. When do I start?" she cheered.

"You start on Monday morning at seven-thirty. Take the weekend off. You will need to be refreshed, ready for your new start."

"Thank you, Sir," Adelia said, hanging up the phone. She made herself dinner and a glass of wine.

In the darkness, lit by only a candle she had made, she thought about her future. Moving her to work across the water could prove expensive for travel. That would mean one thing. She would have to move. She didn't have any family to ask for help from, nor did she have the finance to buy a house. Sighing again, she ate her dinner in silence with the world hanging on her shoulders. "Why oh why, didn't I just keep my mouth shut..." she grumbled. She took another sip of her wine. "There again, it is a promotion, and a pay rise. Perhaps it wouldn't be so bad after all."

Satisfied that her life wasn't going to hell, she finished her pizza and her wine and packed her things. She would spend her weekend house hunting. She looked around at her home, the place where she ate and slept in for almost twenty years. The hard laminate flooring she had laid herself had small gaps around the edges of the rooms. She remembered cursing repeatedly as she tried to make them fit just right. The brown leather sofa was in the centre of the lounge, placed strategically in front of the television with its back to the kitchen. The dark blue lamp shades she despised, brought by her sister, though she couldn't bring herself to say the words. She looked around, lost for words. Even the blinds on the window frame were now faded. It was once pure black and painted with glistening stars with silver paint. It had cost her a pretty penny, and she wasn't ready to let it go.

To live across the water wasn't what she had in mind, but if that was where the boss wanted her, what choice did she have?

Adelia's night filled with the cries of foxes and a sticky heat that made her sweat. She was worried about her future. She turned to face the window, hoping for a cool breeze. The change of locations had come as a surprise, though she was sure that she knew the reason for it.

She got up, licking her lips. Her throat, dry and scratchy from thirst, made it hard to sleep. She walked down her stairs and headed for the kitchen, opened the fridge and reached for a cold bottle of still water. She barely acknowledged the yellow digits on her clock read two twenty-two before turning back to the fridge. The cool air greeted her with a chill.

After taking several large gulps of her drink, she closed the fridge door and carried the water back to the bedroom with her and placed it on the window seal by her head.

The next morning, she woke up earlier than she planned. She went to grab herself some coffee and switched the light on in the still-dark living room. She sat in her favourite chair and contemplated what she was going to do for the day. Looking for a house would be an onerous task, but she wasn't about to give up before she had started. She made a few calls, asking about how much it would take to get her there and back. After the costs for travel and food, her money was sparse and would leave her with less money than what she had started with. Again, she doubted if the promotion was worth the expense and stress. She took a deep breath, carefully lighting a candle with a small match. "It's just temporary," she reminded herself. "Once I move, I will have plenty."

Despite her optimistic comment, her tone was less than convincing, even to her own ears.

The sun rose over the horizon, a small ray of light entered the living room. Adelia sighed, shaking her head. "What have I done?"

She got herself ready, pulled on her coat, and made her way to the car.

Thomas stared at the mirror, frowning. He turned to his wife, holding their six-month daughter. "I just don't know. I can't get my tie on straight," he grumbled. He toyed with the knot of his tie, trying to set it straight and levelling out his tails of the tie, tucking it into his shirt.

"You'll be fine," she laughed. "You've been working there for a while now. I am sure you will do well at the meeting."

He sighed. "It's not just a meeting. There's going to be important clients there, and I don't want to screw up. If I bag this client, for the amount they are asking for, it might finally give me a chance to have a promotion. And Mr Handler is a stickler for details. If I mess up, even a little, it'll be my arse."

"What is the meeting about? Maybe I can help?"

He frowned. "Thanks, but I don't think you can. It's just about finance. We have a great return rate, and always get the money back within the time given. And our motto is a little unusual. We turn no one away. When desperation calls, we deliver."

She frowned back at him, tilting her head a little. "That's a little vague, but I suppose it cuts to the point. Just go to the meeting and tell the truth. That it's a great company, and that they are in very capable hands to give them exactly what they need."

He smiled and kissed her on the cheek. "Exactly what they need might be the way to go. Thanks dear."

He grabbed his keys and took a last look around. Something was still bothering him, though, something that he couldn't shake.

"I am still not sure," he frowned. He could see his wife's long black hair fall past her shoulders.

Her stick-thin frame leaned in and gave him a kiss again. "You'll be fine," she said, assuring him. "Now, Stop fussing," she laughed. "It's the weekend. I am sure you would get the job done. No matter the task."

Monday came with less progress than she had hoped. She woke at four in the morning and got ready to head over to the harbour. The boat was due to arrive at six, and she needed to get to work for seven-thirty. She wondered quietly if there would be a coffee machine on board. She doubted it, but she still hoped.

The boat arrived a little after six. An hour later, she was across the water and standing in an unfamiliar state. The buildings loomed above her. She took out her map on her phone and made her way to Loan Industries.

She arrived, with only minutes to spare. The large white building towered above her, making her feel small and obsolete. She took a deep breath and went inside, hoping to be treated better than the previous sector had treated her. "Ungrateful ingrates," she muttered. She looked around, noting there were very few people inside. She entered the building and made her way to the office. A map on the wall labelled her office on the top floor at the far end of the hall. Smiling, she walked up six flights of stairs and down the hall.

Her office was quite large, with a red rug and her large writing desk. A laptop was on the desk, waiting for her. She smiled, moving it across the room to another table. Then, digging through her work bag, she pulled out her own laptop and placed it in front of her.

Days turned into weeks of quiet solitude. She breathed in the peace and made her way down the stairs. As she entered the hall on the fourth floor, she neared the bottom and stopped. She strained her ears, catching murmured words in whispers. Adelia could just about make out her name, and it wasn't said in light conversation. She frowned, feeling slightly sick. Her new colleagues were conspiring against her!

Not falling for the same crap as before, she decided it was time to do something about it. She hurried down the stairs and headed towards a local electronic shop. Half an hour later, she arrived back at the harbour and headed to her house. If there was going to be a mutiny in the building, she was going to need to know what they were up to. She picked up a small device from her beside the cabinet with a scowl. "I am going to hear everything," she sneered.

Chapter 3

Adelia sat in her office facing her computer, waiting for the rest of her new colleagues to enter the building. She glanced at her bag, sighing. She could still see the receipt from buying some equipment. Adelia cleared her throat, and one by one watched as the workers walked into their office. She stepped out from behind her computer desk and stood at the door. They glanced in her direction and quickly avoided her glare. She shook her head and turned away. She couldn't very well fire the entire building for not liking her. Then again, she supposed there weren't a lot of workers that liked their boss at any job. What was she to do? She faced her computer, slouching back. "Time to get some words done."

On her computer, she typed up the notes on her file. On the files were the addresses and phone numbers of the clients they had. All which had gotten into trouble, and next to their name, was a list of who owed, and what collateral they held against each person. Though they didn't have items to keep, they held something more valuable. Each of them had a secret that would ruin their entire lives with. She cringed. The company specialised in blackmail. Though they weren't paying to keep their mouths shut, they were paying back the money they owed. In her book, though, no matter how you looked at it, it was still blackmail. It was still wrong. She stared out of the window. They wouldn't be so quick to fire her. She knew too much about what was going on, and she knew every little secret about every employee and employer within the company. "Just try it," she muttered. "I can bring them all down to their knees."

"Excuse me, can I speak to you?" a voice asked in a bitter tone.

"What is the problem?" Adelia said. She turned to face a woman with an angry scowl. She had a slender face and a petite frame that looked like a small breeze would knock her over. The woman's long burnt-red hair fell past her shoulders down towards her chest. Her trousers hugged her shapeless legs like twigs peering out from the sleeves. She stood facing her, watching as the woman placed her hands on her non-existent hips.

"We have been talking. We were wondering how long you will stay in this sector for?" the stick woman demanded.

"Crystal, I am here for as long as I need to be. Does anyone have a problem with the way I run this place?"

"No, not at all. We were just wondering. We were doing fine before you came along, that is all."

"According to the records, that isn't quite the truth, is it? Before I came here, you hardly had any customers. Now we do and are making regular income. I assume that you all want to be paid?"

"Yes, but..."

"Then, I suggest you do your job so that I can do mine," Adelia stated with annoyance. "I know that this isn't the ideal way to make money, but it is more effective."

"I... I understand," Crystal replied, defeated. She smoothed down her long black dress and her long blue hair.

Crystal closed the door behind her and left.

Adelia leaned back, watching through a small window as Crystal headed back to her own office cube and spoke to her colleagues. She glanced down at the receipt again. Later, she will listen to whatever was said. She wondered what they were complaining about. It wasn't like they weren't being paid. She shook her head again and waited for the end of the day. Adelia picked up the tape with the recordings on and headed home.

It wasn't like her home across the pond, but her new one-bedroom flat on the second floor was more than enough. She stared out at the water, wishing she were back at her old house. If only she had kept her mouth shut. She wondered what her life would have been like if she hadn't taken the job as a shark loan.

Chapter 4

The next morning, she climbed into her car as she did every morning. Adelia put her mocha into the cup holder and the heating was on full. She shivered, feeling the blast of the crisp cold air that greeted her. She drove away from her block and headed to work. Halfway down the road, she slowed the car to a stop. She took in a deep breath, feeling nauseous. "Do I smell gas?" she wondered, a little worried. She pulled to the side and switched off the engine. Opening the hood of the car, she frowned. She hoped she would see something pointing to the problem of the smell. To her untrained eye, she couldn't see anything. Grumbling, she took out her mobile and gave a mechanic a call. The last thing she needed was a hefty price for repairs. "I am sure it's nothing," she assured herself. She called the mechanic and waited.

She decided it was a good time as any to listen to the recordings from earlier in the day. She clicked the play button and listened intently to the muffled, but familiar voices.

"Something has to be done!" Crystal hissed.

"I know, but what can we do? She is our boss."

"Greg, she wasn't always our boss. How did she get this job?"

"I don't know. The CEO gave it to her from Cylion City."

"Then maybe we can ask them to take her back?"

"For what reason? They won't just take her back just because we don't like her."

"I have an idea," a woman announced. Adelia frowned. The voice sounded familiar. Where did she hear it from? She thought hard, trying to place a face with the voice but come up empty.

There was a brief pause. "How about we simply just get rid of her?"

"Hannah, that is insane. We won't get away with that, can we?"

"Come on? With this many enemies? They wouldn't find out who killed her- especially if we all try."

"I know she's ruthless, but killing her? Isn't that a little extreme?"

"Killing her is the straightforward part. Getting away with it would be much harder. You would have to be clever and remain invisible that no one would give you a second thought," a woman grinned.

"Come on. You know what dirt she has on us. The CEO didn't want her around, either. That is why she's here. She knows too much, and she is ruthless."

"Hence our job description." Crystal commented.

"Yes, to the customers. Not to us! We are supposed to get secrets from the customers to make them pay us back what we owe. Yet, she knows our secrets and what we have all done. Do you trust her to keep that secret? The hell, I don't!"

They looked at each other with a sober expression on their concerned faces. "No. I don't."

"Then I don't see a way out of this. If we are to keep our secrets, we need to kill her, and we need to make sure we burn our secrets out of the system."

"So, how do we do it?" Crystal asked.

"It's best that we don't discuss details. That way, we can't slip up any details."

"Agreed?"

"Agreed," they replied in unison.

Hannah smiled, "Good. Tonight, this week, this month—she will die."

Adelia switched the recording off and thought for a minute, and turned her attention back to the car. If someone had tampered with it, this was more than idle threats. She frowned. "Those backstabbing bitches. They won't get away with this."

A few minutes later, the mechanic arrived and peered into the hood of the car. Not seeing anything of note, the mechanic looked under the car and checked the wiring before climbing out from beneath the vehicle and turning to face her. "Your oil line has a cut. You're lucky that you stopped when you did."

"Let me guess, someone has tampered with my car?" she asked, not really expecting an answer.

"Yeah, actually. Why would someone mess with your car? One little spark and you would have been a goner."

"Ugh. It was a good day to quit smoking then."

"It's a great day to quit. Not smoking just saved your life. How long have you given up for?"

"About a week. I didn't tell anyone, though. I wanted to be smoke free for a few months first before I announce anything."

"You need to call the police about this. I'll get a tow to take the car into evidence."

"Thanks. I'll call them now."

She watched as the mechanic got on to the phone, so she took out hers. "Police please," she told the receptionist. "Someone is trying to kill me."

She arranged a time to make a statement, and the mechanic gave her a lift home. As they reached her front door, she thanked him.

"You never said who was trying to mess with your car?"

"Oh yeah," she sighed. "Someone from work, no doubt. Not sure who, though. I'll find out soon enough."

She said goodbye to the mechanic and went inside. She groaned, stroking her cat as it walked over to greet her. "What a day," she huffed.

The next morning came with the unusual feeling of anticipation. Not the kind she got from working clients, but the kind that makes you wonder what's in the shadows. She poured her coffee into her usual coffee mug and sat down at her table. Having no car to drive to work in meant she now had a choice between walking and getting the bus. She looked outside at the dark grey clouds. "Ah, it is going to piss it down," she noted to herself.

She grabbed her bus pass and headed to the top of her road to wait for the transport to arrive. As usual, it was late.

She climbed onto the bus and went to sit at the back. It was almost empty. On the right was an old woman wearing a yellow coat with silver hair, sitting at the front. Behind her was an elderly man, who was wearing a dark blue jacket and carrying a walking stick. He had thin white hair that looked combed over.

On the right was a woman in her thirties with dark brown hair and a young child covered under the hood of the pram. She smiled as she passed them, and placed herself in the middle of the aisle, at the very back, where she could see everything.

Half an hour later, she finally arrived at her work. She walked in, giving a hard stare at her colleagues, daring them to challenge her. Crystal glanced at her, giving her a puzzled look. "You're late this morning, everything all right?"

"Yes, everything is fine," she lied, smiling. "I thought I might get the bus today and save petrol. It's a little cold out though, kinda wish I brought my car with me. Oh well. What have I missed? New customers?"

"Nothing really. It has been really quiet so far, but we only opened an hour ago."

"Yes, I guess it is a little too early. If there is no one about, you can all have a coffee in the staff room. I can watch out for customers until you're all done."

Crystal gave her another puzzled look and thanked her before walking away.

Adelia smiled, watching as the woman ducked into the staff room with the others. She smirked, watching her colleagues squirm over whether she knew about their plan was priceless. If they had tried to make her car explode, they can squirm all the more. She grinned.

Chapter 5

She glanced down at her draw where the recordings were. She frowned, seeing an opening at the top. The edge of the draw was bent in the corners. She ran her fingers over the indentations. "Someone has been in here," she muttered to herself. "No doubt to get the recording of them." She looked around the room, noting everything else was still tidy. "Strange," she added, amused. She looked along the sides of the room. "They touched nothing else."

She frowned and checked the CCTV cameras around the building. The screen was black. "Damn," she muttered. "Alright. Let's see if they planted anything."

She opened the drawer and stared inside. Inside was a bottle of vodka that she had put there herself. She sighed. Now that she knew they were trying to kill her, she decided not to touch the vodka, after all. She put it to one side. "No point in wasting it," she said to herself. "Maybe someone will get thirsty."

She got on the phone and called the police. "Yes, hello. I have another problem. Someone has been in my office and tampered with a locked draw. They compromised the security cameras. Can you help?"

She waited briefly, waiting as they took down her details. "You'll be over today? That's great news," she finished. She sighed. Her boss would not like this. Adelia got back on the computer and sent her boss overseas an email, telling them of the situation. She opened her mouth to tell them about the attempt on her life. She quickly closed it again. For all she knew, they were in on it.

"It's time to do something about this security problem..." she muttered. She stared at the screen, waiting for the email to come back from the CEO to give her new orders.

She poured herself a coffee and was halfway in drinking it when the computer chimed. "At last." She hurried over to the computer screen.

"I'll send someone else to deal with them. In the meantime, I have emailed another sector, and try to move you. Again. I will have an email sent to you as soon as I hear a reply." She frowned, "Move again? I feel this one won't have as many perks—or maybe I will run the night shift?" she wondered. She grumbled to herself and packed her things away. If they were going to have her killed, they were running out of time. She looked around nervously, knowing full well that this could make them more dangerous. She smiled, glancing back down at the draw. "I think I will leave the Vodka here."

Adele left the building and took her things with her without saying goodbye to the others. She got into her car and headed home, worrying about her future. She had grown accustomed to having a lot of money, but she was thankful to have kept the house across the water from her job. Though, over the last past weeks, she was using it only on the weekends. She sighed and headed back to the place she knew so well. The familiar roads greeted her with the usual crowd, all in a hurry to get places, whether it was to go to work or head home for lunch. The cars beeped, lights flashed, and the drivers bellowed at each other to "Get out of the Way!"

She made her way to the front door and let herself in. She let out her cat from its carrier to get used to the familiar surroundings again before going back to sleep. The sky had already darkened, and the clouds covered what few stars were twinkling in the twilight sky. She could smell the kebabs and chips coming from across the block behind her. She smiled. It had been a while since she treated herself. "Why not?" she mused, deciding. She picked up the phone, ordered her dinner, and went over to the fridge. Smiling, she reached to the far back of the top shelf and pulled out a bottle of red wine. "I needed this," she sighed. "I don't know how much longer I can do this for. They are really trying to test my temper." She turned to her cat, who was curled up into a tight ball.

She ate her dinner and was about to run her bath when the computer chimed. She sighed and opened up her emails. One of the CEO was waiting for her. She held her breath and read. "Thankfully, there's another sector in this area, but it is a bit of a distance. Much like across the water. This one, though, is further up, past the countryside and across the Bramble Village Bridge. It is small, and there are very few customers. It is a good place to lie low, and there should be no trouble. You start on Thursday. I am sure you can get there by car, and it shouldn't take you more than a couple of hours to drive each way. Regards, Johnson. CEO of Loan Industries."

Chapter 6

Thursday came with dark grey skies. Adelia left in her car, putting in a full tank of petrol, and made her way to the new building. She was relieved that it covered the expenses within the costs, though she wasn't thrilled to have to be driving for four hours each day. She passed the sea and then passed the bridge and halfway up to the other side of the country. Grumbling, she arrived at her destination. She looked at the small dingy building, wiping the grim off the front door with her sleeves. "Anyone in?" she called out. With having no one answering, she used the key that they sent her in the mail, and went inside. Inside, they covered the furniture with sheets. The floor was dusty. The windows had a thick layer of dust and dirt. She pressed her lips tightly together. Something was not right. She looked around, hoping for an explanation. Inside, on the table, was an envelope with her name written on it. "This is a new building. Well, new to us. I bought this recently. Please have everything cleaned ready to do business in. We are opening this place up in three weeks. You are on your own, so there is no one to piss off. Perhaps this will encourage you to think about how useful you can be to this company in the future."

Adelia swallowed hard and looked around. Three weeks. It was an impossible task. Yet, she was expected to pull off a miracle. This wasn't a promotion. This was punishment. "I did nothing wrong! I'm supposed to be good at what I do. It's my job! I find out information, and now I'm demoted to a fucking janitor?!" she growled, scrunching the letter into a paper ball. "Of all the things I have done for this company? This is bullshit!"

She looked around at what the last owners had left in the building, wondering how she could profit from this disaster. Underneath the sheets were some equipment, double boilers, glass jars, wicks and clips and some wax. On a shelf were some scented oils. Adelia gasped, "This is awesome. The last owner must have been a candle maker. I love candles!" she cheered excitedly. "Finally, something good has come out of this. I can take these home and make my own candles. So many scents to try..." she said, beaming. She looked around again. "This is the best day ever!"

Rummaging through the cupboards, she dug out some wax, some food colouring and some oils. She switched on the power and grinned. She left the lights on as she carried the equipment out to her car. After a few trips, she went back inside and cleaned the floors and the windows to get ready for business. She swept the cobwebs from the corners, coated the surfaces with bleach and then made her way to each room. Scrubbing the surfaces and wiping away the black grime, she thought about the wax in the car and what colours and scents she could create. Her eyes darted to the clock, eager to get home and experiment. She sighed, wiping the sweat from her brow. Just as she was about to have her lunch, her phone rang.

"Hello?" she greeted.

"How is it looking?" a voice asked.

"Mr Johnson, sir. It is looking better. I've cleaned the windows, cleared the room and it just needs a deep clean now."

"No trouble?"

"Well, no one can give me trouble. There isn't anyone here," she retorted.

"Good. I am sure you will be happy to stay there for a while then."

"On my own? Are you serious?" she asked. "How would I get paid? Via the bank?"

"I thought you would have worked that out yourself. No customers, no payments."

"So, I've been cleaning for free?" She hissed, growing more agitated. "Look at it like an investment. Once it's open for business, you'll get paid when the customers roll in."

"That could take months!" she gasped, horrified.

"Perhaps."

She closed her eyes and took a deep breath. She snapped her eyes open, grinding her teeth. "You know what, Mr Johnson. I ain't no skivvy. You want this place cleaned up, do it your damn self! I quit!"

"You're still on contract," he growled. "Remember?"

"Screw your contract. You didn't want me here anymore, anyway. You wanted me out, you've got it. I'm out."

"You know, you know too much." Mr Handler stated in a warning tone.

"Yes. I know of a lot about everyone. Don't worry, I'll keep my mouth shut as long as everyone leaves me alone."

"Fine, fine. You can come and get the last of your pay from me personally. And then you can announce that you quit to the entire company."

"And be your entertainment? I'm not stupid. I'll come and say goodbye. There are a few people I have unfinished business with."

She grabbed the key, closed the door behind her, and looked around. Seeing no one around, she snapped the key in the lock with a grin. "Now try to get in, bastards."

Chapter 7

A delia stood at the entrance of the building of where she had spent many years of her life. She sighed irritably and went inside to give the workers the ultimate gift. Something that would be a reminder of the years she had given them. The workers were not due to arrive for almost an hour. She took out her bag and placed a small box on each of the desks. She needn't put a name on them, certain that they would know who the present was from. It wasn't like the others would give out gifts. She shrugged to herself. She didn't care either way. They would know soon enough.

After finishing the task, she left the building and handed the rest of the presents to the rest of the company. And then, for good measure, sent the remaining company buildings the same present. "I wouldn't want to be accused of not being fair," she commented to herself.

An hour later, she headed home and tidied her house. She had not been home for long enough to do any cleaning, but now she had more than enough time. Eager to get started, she grabbed her gloves, preparing to deep-clean every surface of the house. Taking a deep breath, she switched on some music and got to work.

A few days passed, the weather continued to cool to almost freezing, and the frost on the ground got a little crispy.

Joe stood at his kitchen unit, hunched over the almost boiling kettle. The distinct odour from the coffee filled the room as it had every morning for the last twenty years. This was not his first cup of the morning, though, nor was it his second. He could hear the television in the background. The news was on. There had been a power cut the night before, but no one knew what had caused it yet and the electricians were investigating the problem. He shrugged. He was in bed, so it hadn't affected him. The kettle switched off with a click, breaking his train of thought. Joe filled his cup and poured in a small splash of milk before making his way over to his dining table. In front of him was his laptop, a scented candle and the newspaper. Placing his mug down in front of him, Joe prepared for his morning routine. Before heading out to work, he browsed through the social media and checked his email. He put on his suit, fastened his tie and knotted his laces. He slipped on his leather coat, grabbed his keys, and went back to finish the emails. The computer needed updating, and the loading time had slowed down to a crawl. He sighed. By the time he got himself ready, the page had loaded up and ready. He flicked through the pages, noting that two of his friends had a new baby, and another had a new job. "Congrats on the new arrival," he typed. Then commented on the next. "Congrats on the new job." He smiled before adding another comment. "I've got a new mug!" he cheered, posting a picture of his white coffee mug with a picture of a zombie printed on the front.

"Anything interesting?" his wife asked. He turned around to face her. She was looking as beautiful as ever, if not a little tired. She had long black hair with brown hazel nut eyes, wrapped in a light pink dressing gown.

"Not really, Babe. The usual crap. Babies and new career mile stones. I've just joined in the celebrating by telling them about my new mug."

"But you got that mug three months ago," she retorted with a puzzled frown.

"Yeah, but they don't know that," he chirped. "It is still kinda new."

"Don't forget about your doctor appointment this afternoon," she reminded him gently.

"Oh. Right. I suppose," he huffed.

"You knew it was today. You made the appointment weeks ago."

"Yeah, but it is only for a health check, and I'm fine."

"You can tell me you're fine after the doctor gives you the all clear."

"I will, as soon as I have finished the appointment."

"Oh no," she chuckled. "I am coming with you to make sure you go. The doctor can tell me you're fine."

"Really? You don't need to hold my hand, Megan. I am a grown man."

"A grown man who is as stubborn as a two-year-old at bedtime," she grinned. "Come on, it is time to go."

Joe grumbled and reluctantly agreed. He switched off the computer. He stood up, put his laptop away, and followed his wife to the car.

"This is a bad idea," he stated irritably.

They arrived at the doctor's office with a few minutes to spare. They glanced at the rows of seats at the end of the room and reluctantly picked a seat at the back.

After waiting for almost fifteen minutes, Joe was called in to the office. The doctor sat next to a desk facing a computer, reading the medical record on the monitor. "What can I do for you?" the doctor asked, turning to face them.

"I am here for a health check," he replied, folding his arms defensively.

"Alright. We'll start with your pulse," the doctor smiled. Next, he checked his heart rate and then moved on to the blood pressure. He wrapped a Velcro fabric around his arm and tightened the strap. He took it off and wrote the results.

"What's the news, doc?" he chuckled. "I am fine, right?" he turned to his wife, puffing up his chest. "See. I said I was fine."

"Actually, your blood pressure is really high. Do you drink a lot of caffeine? Energy drinks and coffee, etc?"

"Uh, maybe?" he murmured.

"With it being this high, I am going to have to give you an instruction you will not like."

"Uh, what? I don't like the sound of that. I get enough exercise. It's not as if I am a couch potato."

"No, but you have too much caffeine. How much coffee and energy drinks do you have each day?"

"I drink around eight coffees and maybe three energy drinks a day."

"Yeah, way too much. Until your blood pressure returns to a normal rate, you are going to have to give up caffeine. Give it two weeks and then come back and we'll check your blood pressure again. Until then, no caffeine. Drink decaf tea or coffee, maybe some water too, to keep you hydrated instead of those energy drinks."

"Give up Caffeine? Are you serious?" he demanded, pleading with him.

"Yes. Unless you would like to have a heart attack?"

"No, I don't want to have a heart attack. But, do I really need to give up caffeine? Maybe I can just cut down on my energy drinks, to one a day?"

"Look, get your blood pressure back to normal. No caffeine for two weeks. If your blood pressure is at a good rate, you can to have one energy drink a day, and only four cups of coffee a day. Any more than that, and you would have to give up, permanently."

Joe swallowed hard. "So, two weeks with no caffeinated drinks? I am sure I can survive that... I hope."

They left the office, with Megan following him out with a smug smile. "Aren't you glad I took you down there?"

"Actually, no." he grunted. "I really wish you hadn't."

"Come on, it's not that bad," she smiled, nudging him.

"Not that bad? Have you seen how much coffee I drink before work in the mornings?"

"I don't know. A large?" she frowned.

"And the rest. I wake up and have two coffees before I get dressed. And then after I am dressed, I have another two. I drink two coffees at a time. And I drink over eight."

"Yeah, I thought that was on the light side of the scale."

"I drink fifteen cups a day, and that is without the four energy drinks."

"And you wonder why you're constipated all the time? Fuck sake, Joe. You're gonna kill yourself!"

"Trust me, babe. It is not the caffeine that's going to kill me. It'll be the lack of it. Just you watch."

"You're such a drama queen. You'll be fine. Tonight you'll sleep well, and then tomorrow you'll feel great."

"We'll see," he grumbled, "But I ain't convinced."

They got home and switched on the television. She watched her shows, and he sat back at the laptop to re-check his emails. He sighed. He knew she meant well. Though, this was one of those days where he wished she could care for him a little less. He frowned, shaking his head. Maybe not less, but not as concerned about his health. It wasn't like he was ill or anything.

They ate their spaghetti bolognese in silence that night, and he went to bed early. Not having caffeine was already proving to be difficult, and the fatigue was already mocking him. He glanced at the clock. It was barely ten. He sighed, went up to his bedroom, and switched on the lamp. Maybe a good book would distract him from the coffee.

The morning came with an unwelcome glare as it beamed through his bedroom window. He yawned and slowly sat up in his bed. Megan was still sleeping soundly beside him. Careful not to wake her, Joe climbed out of bed and made his way to the kitchen. He took out his zombie cup and reached for the coffee machine. He blinked, remembering what his doctor had ordered. No caffeine. "Shit," he cursed, banging his head against the cupboard door. "Now how am I gonna wake up?" He looked through the fridge and checked behind the bottles of water and the block of cheese and packets of cooked ham. Resigning to whatever was left of the beverages, he picked up a small bottle of orange and poured some into a glass, then topped it up with iced water from the fridge. He gulped it down, screwing his face with disgust, sticking his tongue out. "Ugh, vile stuff." he spat. "That did the job for the minute, I guess."

He pulled out one of his bottles of water and put it into his backpack, ready to take to work, making a mental note to himself to buy some more.

Chapter 8

The nurse sat behind the desk of the hospital, scanning through the files on the computer. The queue was getting longer by the minute, and the patients were growing a little agitated. "Next please," she called out, signalling the front of the line. "How can we help you today?"

"Hi," a woman groaned. "I am not feeling too well."

"Name?" she huffed. "And symptoms please?"

"My name is Amy. I feel sick and cramping up. I don't feel right."

"It sounds like the bug. I'll send you round to the out of office doctors, and they can help you."

"Thank you," she sobbed, clutching her stomach. Swear poured from her forehead, drenching her hair line. She shuddered. "I don't like this bug. I have never had it this bad before."

"I am sure you will be alright soon." She moved the patient on and signalled the next person in the line.

"How can I help you today?" she repeated.

"I am not sure. It's strange. I don't feel well. I keep getting these cramps and feels like a bug..." she explained. "But I am pretty sure the bug doesn't do this," she frowned, looking very pale. She reached up to the top of her head and pulled out a fist full of hair. "It's been like this for days. I... I think I have cancer!"

The nurse frowned, looking concerned. Her brows folded as though she were inspecting something under extreme scrutiny. "Take a seat. The wait may be a while, though." She sighed. "What's your name?"

"My name is Crystal." she replied. "What's yours?"

"Helen," she said. "Please take a seat, Crystal. A doctor will see you soon."

Crystal went to sit down, moving her legs as stiff as sticks. She slowly picked a seat at the front of the room and looked around at the rest of the people waiting. Some looked drunk, and others looked like they had a nasty fall. In the far corner was a familiar face.

"Amy?" she greeted, smiling weakly. "What are you doing in this place?"

"I don't feel well. Nurse thinks it is a bug," she sobbed.

"I don't think this is a bug, mate. You look how I feel. But at least you're not losing your hair," she smiled.

"What?" Amy gasped, "What do you mean this isn't a bug? Is it serious? Am I dying?" she asked, her voice became panicked and shrill.

Crystal cleared her throat, trying to think of how to calm her friend down. "The losing hair might just be me. I think I have cancer. Pretty sure that it isn't contagious. How long have you been unwell?"

"A few days," she groaned. "I can't seem to shift it. You?"

"A couple of weeks. I can't shift mine either. Figured the hospital should look."

"Wise choice," Amy agreed. "I hope we get sorted soon. We're heading over to the new sector next week. Boss wants it immaculate before we look for more clients."

"Which sector is that?" Crystal asked, intrigued.

"Up at the other side of the state."

"Hey, isn't that the one that what's-her-name went to before she quit?"

Amy blinked, thinking back. "You know what? I think you're right. Good thing I am not going alone. I am not ready to leave the company yet. I like my job."

"Money and secrets. What's there not to like?" Crystal grinned.

After hours of waiting, Amy was the first to be seen. After a hurried checkup, they promptly sent her home with a few paracetamol tablets and instructed to take a few days to rest. Crystal was next, forcing herself to take each step towards the office.

"What can we do for you?" the nurse asked softly.

"Um, looks like a bug—except for my hair falling out," Crystal explained. "I feel rough, I've lost weight, I have the runs, vomiting and cramps. I either have the worst bug in history or I have cancer."

"Alright. We'll do a blood test and run some scans to have a look."

"Thank you," she sighed. She blinked, shaking her head. "Do you have a bucket? I am going to be sick again."

The nurse handed her a cardboard bowl and watched as Crystal went into the toilet. A few moments later, she exited the toilet, frowning more. "I don't think I have the bug. I have blood in my pee."

"Blood in your pee? Are you sure?"

Crystal nodded. The nurse frowned, looking around before signaling another nurse to approach her. "Please take her to another room. She has blood in her urine. I want to check her for kidney problems. Could be very serious."

The nurse nodded, looking at the patient with a small smile. "Come on, let's find out what is making you feel poorly."

Crystal nodded, biting her lip. "I would appreciate it."

After running some tests, the nurses lead her into a ward. She entered a small room with a bed and a bedside cabinet. On the side was a plastic cup and some iced water. "You can stay here for the night, and we'll pop in and monitor your condition."

"Alright. Thank you. Is it OK for me to have a cup of tea, please?" Crystal asked, smiling.

She nodded, "Yes, alright. I'll bring you one right over before I check on the other patients."

Chapter 9

J oe sat at his dining table, staring down at his bowl of cereal and his morning drink. He grumbled to himself, before swallowing a large mouthful of his juice. "Ugh. I hate juice," he complained. "How many more days have I got until I can start having coffee again?"

Megan looked at him with a smile. "About a week and three days," she replied. "Don't you feel better about it yet?"

"No, I don't," he huffed. "I feel tired all the damn time. I want my coffee."

She turned away and headed towards the kitchen. "I'll make you a small cup," she commented. "Only a small one, though."

He smiled, "Thank you!"

She switched on the kettle and took out a jar of coffee that she had bought just days before. Smirking, she ripped off the label on the jar, disposing of the word 'Decaf' printed at the bottom. She made his coffee how he liked it, and then walked it over to him and placed it on the table beside his bowl. "Don't worry, I won't tell the doctor you gave it to me. He won't notice one cup."

"Oh, I know. Just don't overdo it when you get his permission."

"OK. I lo-"

His phone rang loudly, vibrating against the wooden surface of the table. He frowned, answering it with a yawn. "Hello?"

He listened to the caller, his expression became hard and irritated. "Alright. I will be right there."

"What's wrong?" she asked him, concerned.

"I'll have to drink my coffee on the go. Someone has discovered a body. A woman."

"That's awful."

"Yes. I have got to go." He poured his coffee into a travel mug and quickly got ready to go. He kissed his wife on the lips and left in a hurry.

He arrived at the house, with the coroner standing by the front door. "Hiya. What have we got?" Joe asked.

"It looks like a poisoning, but I can't see anything on him to suggest a struggle or that she had anyone here with her. It's all yours now."

"How long ago did she die?" Joe enquired, getting out his notebook.

"I would say around three hours ago. I'll have to do an autopsy before I can say anything else, though."

"Alright. Thank you."

He looked walked into the house and looked around.

The breakfast bowl was still out and only half eaten. She had drunk almost all of her coffee with only the last few mouthfuls at the bottom of the cup. "Can someone collect the drink and whatever is in the breakfast bowl, please? Perhaps it was in her breakfast?"

He turned his attention to the kitchen. It was small with an L shaped unit. The fridge was bare other than a few essentials. "No sign of having company," he noted. He walked through the room and went towards the living room. Inside the living room was a large black corner sofa with a coffee table in the center of the room. A television was hanging on the wall at the far end. Underneath the tv was a black glass table. He went in for a closer look. He could see a pile of books on one side, at the bottom shelf, sitting on a pile of magazines. On the top shelf was another book, though he couldn't work out the name on the cover without disturbing the evidence. On the other side of the book was a glass candle that had almost burnt out with a wooden wick. He smiled, recognising the scent of Wild Jasmine and Vanilla. Sighing again, there was still no sign of company. He made a note in his book and moved on to the bedroom. There, he could see a large queen sized bed, with a large four-door wardrobe.

With nothing to learn, he decided it was time to tell the family the bad news. "Do we have a name yet?" Joe asked.

"Yes. Her name is Amy Price. She was 23 years old."

"Damn. That's young. Alright, send me the address of her parents and I'll tell them the bad news. In the meantime, check the bathroom for signs of having company or drugs- and find out where the poison came from."

They looked through her phone and scanned the contacts for emergency contacts. At the top of the list were the details of her mother, father, and their address.

Joe sighed. This was the worst part of the job, but in this career, it was a necessary step to catch the killer.

He typed the address into his SATNAV and started the car.

"Wait up!" a voice cried out.

He turned to his right, seeing a man jog towards him. "I am coming with you. I'm Detective Bells." Derek said, holding out his hand.

"Hello, Detective Bells. I take it the boss sent you to be my partner for this case?"

"Yes. I literally just missed you. I was having a look in the garden. Did you see their pond?"

"Can't say I have," he replied. "Was it anything of importance?"

Derek shrugged his shoulders. "I thought it would be an ideal source of poison. Since we don't know what poisoned her yet. I took a sample and gave it to the forensics to test."

"Good thinking," Joe smiled. "Now for the hard part. Telling the parents that they just lost a daughter."

"I won't stop you. I just hope that we catch whoever did this."

"So do I."

They arrived at the house and parked the car. The house was fairly big and stony. The front of the house was peeling, flecks of white paint speckled across the walls. Clearing his thoughts, Joe stepped out of the car and approached the front door. The red door had a brass knocker pinned to the top center between two small windows. He gave three hard knocks and looked around.

"Hang on, I'm coming," an elderly woman's voice called out.

"Take your time," Joe called back.

After a few moments of waiting, a frail-looking woman opened the front door. "What can I do for you, gentlemen?" she asked.

Joe stepped back, so that the woman wouldn't feel intimidated. "I'm Detective Hansel. This is my colleague, Detective Bells Andrews. I don't suppose we can come in? I'm afraid I have some bad news."

"Uh, sure. Would you like a drink? I've just made a fresh pot of coffee." the woman offered.

"Uh..." Joe took a deep breath in, his eye twitched. "N... No thank you."

Derek looked at him with a puzzled frown. "Uh, I wouldn't mind a glass of water, if it isn't too much trouble?"

The woman nodded, making her way to the kitchen sink and poured some water in to a glass of ice. She handed Derek the glass, and he thanked her with a little smile. "Now, what's this about having some bad news?"

"Right..." Joe murmured. "We found a body. We believe it belongs to Amy."

"Not my Amy? You must be mistaken."

"I am really sorry. Do you have a picture of her for confirmation?" Joe asked, prompting her.

The woman nodded, quickly getting out of her seat.

She went into the kitchen and returned with a large photo album.

She flicked through a few pages before pulling out a photo of a young woman with bright orange hair and a red jeans and a black top. Joe sighed. Other than the apparent hair dye, this was the same person as the victim that laid in the morgue.

"It's a mistake, see?" she said, sounding hopeful. She watched as his expression saddened. She swallowed hard, straightening her back to brace herself. "Right? Tell me you have made a mistake!"

He looked at her, a hard lump formed in his suddenly dry throat. "I can't," he said in a hoarse voice. "I am sorry. But this only proves that the person we found is Amy. They found her at her address... it's her."

"But, how? How did she die? She's healthy, she is not a smoker or takes drugs, exercises regularly..."

"Someone poisoned her," Joe replied. "Do you know if there was anyone she was having trouble with?"

She buried her face in her hands, sobbing uncontrollably. Tears streamed down her face. "No. She was a lovely girl. She wouldn't harm a fly- never said a bad word about anyone."

"I'm sorry for your loss," Derek said sadly.

"But... It's my daughter. My only child! Who took her from me?" she wept.

"That's what we're going to find out."

Her expression hardened. "Everything I had to live for is gone. I have no one left... What do you need?"

"We'll need a list of friends, co-workers, other family members..."

"Alright. I'll get you a list," she growled. "The murderer won't get away with this."

"We will hold the murderer accountable, if we can help it."

"Good. I want the killer to die for taking my baby!"

She handed them the list of her family members and what few friends Amy had.

Derek sighed, putting the list in with the pages of his notebook. "Can we look in Amy's room? Maybe she wrote something down somewhere that might show any problems she might have had? Maybe a boyfriend or fallen out with someone?"

"Help yourself," she gestured. "It is upstairs, first door on the left."

Joe thanked her and climbed the stairs.

The bedroom was fairly small, nothing more than a slightly larger box room.

The woman walked in behind him. "She has her own place now, so she doesn't come in very often. I touch nothing though, in case she comes back. Now she never will..." she cried. "I was going to give her this house- but now even that is gone."

The Detectives sighed, unable to make the words come out. "I am really sorry," Joe muttered. "We will do our best to find who did this, I swear it."

"Thank you. But swearing isn't gong to give my daughter her life back. I want the killer brought to justice- make the killer pay. Or I will use the rest of what I have left of my life, tracking the killer down myself!"

"You can't make threats like that," Derek whispered.

"I just did," she growled. "Not only will I track the killer down, I'll make them swallow whatever they killed my daughter with. I don't care if it takes every breath I have. I am going to avenge my Amy."

Chapter 10

J oe looked at the body, waiting for the medical examiner to finish her report. "What poisoned her?" he frowned.

"Arsenic," she replied, not taking her eyes off her work.

"Really? How? Did she ingest it?"

Sian shook her head, then flicked her black hair out of the way from her face. "No. She has been inhaling it. It looks like it was taking a while as well. Maybe it leaked into her room whilst she was sleeping?" she mused.

He sighed. "Yes, I suppose she could have. But I saw nothing they could leak it from."

"Maybe through a tube under the door? The medical records say she went to hospital a few days ago complaining of bug like symptoms and got sent home with paracetamol and rest. Clearly, it wasn't a bug."

"Was there anything to suggest when she got it?"

She looked at her results and thought for a moment. "It looks like they did it in stages—so maybe someone close to her had frequent visits in order to dose her up. It doesn't look like she was smoking. So maybe it was in an air freshener of some sort."

He sighed, "It's going to be one of those cases that is going to keep me up at night, isn't it?"

"It is looking that way, yes. I can prescribe some sleeping pills if you struggle too much?"

"Thanks Sian. I will let you know."

Joe walked out of the autopsy room and went to the car where Derek was waiting. "How did it go?"

"They killed her with arsenic. Inhaled it. Maybe we are looking for an air freshener with a home made canister of some sort. Or look again for somewhere a tube might have fitted under a door or through a window?"

"Damn. Alright. Thinking of going back to the crime scene, then?"

"That's the plan. And we need to find out who would want to poison her."

The Detectives headed back to the crime scene and let themselves in. The tape was still going around the house. They ducked under the taping and went through the front door.

Inside, the house was dark. Joe went to switch the lights on, but to no avail. He grunted to himself, wishing that he had a cup of coffee to heat him up in this cold. "Why is everything turned off?" he grumbled.

"It must be another power cut," Derek huffed. "The winds keep knocking the power lines. I think they should get fixed again this afternoon?"

"This happens a lot?" Joe wondered.

"Just a couple of times," he replied. "It doesn't last long though, thankfully."

"i hope it don't mess with mine. I have food in the fridge that needs to be cooked for my dinner tonight."

"It will probably be fine," Derek laughed.

"I hope so. It is bad enough that I have to go without my coffee for a while. I am not losing my dinner as well."

"Not drinking coffee? Is that why you turned it down? Why are you not drinking coffee?"

"So many questions at once!" Joe grumbled. "Pick one!"

"All of them," he grinned.

"My blood pressure is too high. Doctor has ordered me to stop drinking caffeine until he is happy with the numbers."

"How are you handling it?"

"Not great. It's my third day. I can't even have energy drinks! I am stuck with juice and bloody water for at least a month."

"That's harsh. Hopefully, you won't have to wait it out too long."

"You're telling me," Joe agreed. He looked at the doors separating the rooms and looked down at the carpet. "There doesn't seem to be enough of a gap to get a tube in underneath."

"What about in the hinges?" Derek asked.

Joe had a closer look. There was no indentation or transfer, or any residue. "It doesn't look like it. Maybe they got in through the window? You check the kitchen for air fresheners to see if any of them have arsenic in the ingredients."

"Would that even be legal?"

"I wouldn't be sure either way. Who actually looks at those?"

They checked round the other doors with a sigh. "This is tedious. There is nothing there- it must be something else."

"That is a good point. Maybe she got poisoned at work?"

Joe thought for a moment. "Nice call out," he cheered. "Lets find out if there is anything at her office to poison her. Maybe the air freshener is at work, or the tubes residue around her area. Something has got to be giving out fumes."

"Where does she work?" Derek asked. "I don't think I saw anything written about that."

"Loan industries or something like that, I believe. I have written the address down, anyway."

"Awesome. Let's have a look then. I hope they serve food..."

"It's a loan place, not a restaurant," Joe muttered. He looked down at the time on his watch. "But it has gone lunch time. Why not grab a burger on the way down there?"

"Sounds like a brilliant plan," Derek cheered. "A cheese burger sounds fantastic round about now."

Joe agreed and climbed into his car. Derek followed behind him, getting secured I his seat whilst joe put the heating on. He shivered against the icy cold air. "Damn, it is freezing today," he complained.

"Yep. Winter has officially arrived. I can't feel my feet."

They arrived almost half an hour later. Inside the building, there were sofas in the waiting area, and the desks had a computer on each. Rows of ten lined the room with each cubicle. "Which one do you think is Amy's?" Joe wondered.

Derek shrugged. "This place looks like a maze. Do you think anyone gets lost finding their desks?"

It was almost five minutes of waiting before someone approached them. "What can we do for you?" a voice greeted from behind them.

"We are here about Amy. I assume that you have heard what has happened by now?"

"No, what is the problem? Is she in trouble?"

"You could say that," Derek said. "She's dead."

"What?! How'd this happen?"

"Poison. We couldn't see anything at her house that may have been the source, so we thought we would check her office."

"It is in the third one on the right. Next to the small window."

The Detectives thanked the man in the grey suit and turned around. "What's your name?" Joe asked, suddenly remembering his lines.

"Carl Handler," he replied. "I am the manager of this building."

"Alright. I am going to need everything she was working on in case someone was being a difficult customer."

"We don't get difficult customers, they appreciate our help. But very well, I will get you what you need."

"Thank you," Joe smiled.

The office didn't look like much. The cubicle next to her office door blocked most of the view. They opened the door and went inside for a look around. "There must be something here," Joe whispered to himself. "She can't have got poisoned from nothing. There has to be something I'm missing."

Derek looked in the drawers, whilst Joe looked through the cupboards. "Paper and files," Derek sighed. "I am seeing nothing useful. Not even a spray of deodorant or even a can of hair spray. There is nothing here."

Grumbling, Joe massaged his temples, feeling a headache emerging behind his eyes. "This is going to be a long and tedious investigation, isn't it?" he huffed.

"You have already said this, and yes, the answer is still yes. It is certainly looking like it is going to take us a while to sort this out one. Murders are so messy usually, but this one is really clean. A clean murder. I didn't think I would see one that doesn't have blood."

"There are strangulations," Joe reminded him.

"Oh yeah, I suppose. But we don't hear about that one very often either. It is all stabbing and shootouts."

Joe's phone rang. He answered the phone and sighed. "I need you to come asap," he was told, with no introduction. There was no need. It was the doctors they had spoken to earlier. He dragged his hand down his face, groaning. There was another body waiting for them. "Shit," he grumbled.

"What the fuck happened now?" Derek frowned, watching as Joe's expression darkened.

Joe hung up the phone and turned to his partner. "We have to go back to the hospital. There's been another victim. It is another woman."

A few of the workers looked up with interest and worry, but said nothing. They showed themselves out of the building and made their way to the car. "A very tedious case," he repeated. "I knew it."

Chapter 11

They arrived at the hospital and made their way over to the ward where Crystal's body was waiting. Joe frowned, looking down at the body of the young woman. "You said her name was Crystal. Do you know her last name?"

"Yes. Her last name is Jones. Crystal Jones. She lives in a house near to the town centre, according to her files."

"OK. Was the medical examiner called?"

"Yes, she is on her way down now. She had to get the room ready and sterilised before coming." the nurse explained.

"Thank you, nurse Anderson. You have been a great help. Can you tell me what happened leading up to the time she died?"

"Yeah, she came in complaining of cramps and bug like symptoms, but her hair was also falling out. She was concerned. Then she went to the toilet and said that she had blood in her urine. So we kept her in for observation. She died sometime this morning or during the night. We found her dead this morning." Nurse Anderson explained.

Joe nodded, writing her words down on his writing pad.

"Was there anyone else that had these symptoms?" he prompted.

The nurse shrugged. "The bug has been going round for a few weeks. This is the first one that has died from this."

"Alright. I am sure the medical examiner will confirm my suspicion, but I think maybe she got poisoned like the others."

"Poisoned by what?" the nurse frowned. "Crystal came in thinking that she had cancer."

"Yeah, it is not cancer," Joe sighed. "If my hunch is right, then it is murder."

A few moments later, the medical examiner entered the room with her bag. She looked at the body, examining her carefully before moving the body and getting the temperature probe out.

She checked her nails and her hair and sighed. "There are white lines on her nails. She has definitely got poisoned. I'll have to do a blood test, though, to confirm which poison. My prognosis, though, is that it is the same poison that killed your other victim."

"Thanks, Sian. I appreciate it."

"Just doing my job. I'll meet you back at the morgue when I have finished doing the autopsy."

Joe nodded again and sighed. "What time would you say she died?"

"Temperature and rigor mortis puts her at 11:20 this morning," she replied.

He cleared his dry throat and had a sip of his bottled water.

"No energy drink today?" Sian teased.

He shook his head. "No. My GP says that my blood pressure is too high. I have to cut out my caffeine until it goes back to normal."

"Yikes. Well, I will let you get on with it then."

He thanked her and left, turning to his colleague, Derek.

"Come on. Time to let the family know. It's your turn this time."

Sian handed Joe the address to Crystal's parents and went back to work.

Joe grumbled as he left the hospital building with a worried look on his face. "This is the second murder within days. And we still don't know who or how they are getting poisoned. There has to be something..." he blinked. "They both drive, don't they?"

Derek shrugged. "Yeah, I think so. Why?"

"What if the poison is in the car? We'll have their cars towed and brought to evidence. Perhaps the poison is getting in from the Air conditioning... that would explain the gradual exposure to it."

"That's a good idea. I will call them now."

Derek made the call to the town people and stared out of the passenger window, watching the streets pass them by as they made their way to the family home. He swallowed hard. "Are you sure that you want me to break the news? I never know what to say," he asked, whining.

"Yes, I will not be the only one with the bad news. It is your turn."

Derek agreed with reluctance and went back to stare out of the window. He frowned. "What am I going to say?"

"Just say the usual," Joe assured him. "Look, if you are really that desperate, I will break the news. OK?"

Derek looked at him and nodded. His shoulders sagged as the relief lifted his stress away. "You're a good man," he smiled.

Joe agreed and went back to concentrating on his driving. After passing three roundabouts and a cross junction, they finally arrived at the family home where Crystal had lived.

Derek walked up to the front porch and knocked loudly, holding his breath. The front door had two windows, ice covered the glass. He shoved his icy stiff hands back into his pockets and shivered.

Joe watched with a smirk. He could see Derek flexing his fingers through the thick green coat. "Are you cold enough?" he chuckled.

Almost two minutes later, the door opened.

"Hello. Can I help you?" a woman asked. She had blonde hair with ginger highlights.

"Are you Mrs Jones?" Derek asked.

"Yes. Who are you?"

Joe stepped beside Derek with an outreached hand. "My name is Detective Twit, and this is Detective Bells. May we come inside? It's bitter cold out and we have a couple of questions."

The woman moved aside and allowed the Detectives into her house. "What is it you want to ask?"

"Sit down," Derek suggested nervously.

"No, I'll stand. Please, what is it you want to ask?"

"Uh... Crystal is..." Derek began, struggling to get his words out.

Joe placed a hand on his colleagues's shoulder. "I am really sorry, but Crystal went to the hospital last night with some complaints."

"Crystal? What complaints? Is she alright?"

"She was not feeling her best. I am afraid to say she has passed away."

"That can't be right. She is only in her thirties. How? Was she sick?"

"Uh, no. Someone... killed her."

The woman blinked, tears welled up in her eyes. She cleared her throat and tried blinking the tears away. "Murdered? How? And who by? Have you got the killer?"

"I am sorry about this. Really, I am, and I know this is hard. Someone poisoned her. Please, when was the last time you saw her?"

The mother's knees buckled as she collapsed on to the floor, gasping for breath. She held her chest, clutching at her clothes. Her ragged breaths turned into heavy sobs of despair. "My poor baby. My poor child. Who could do such a thing?"

She looked up, red-faced, and her red swollen eyes looked back at them. "Did she suffer?"

"No, she didn't suffer. She didn't even realise it was happening." Derek lied. It was the least he could do to reassure the grieving family. He had this conversation more times than he would care to.

"The last time you spoke to her, did she mention having trouble with anyone? Perhaps someone at work? Or an ex?"

"Not to my knowledge. She enjoyed her work, and she hasn't been seeing anyone for almost two years. I just... I don't know how someone can do this to her. She was a sweet girl, always smiled and lent a hand..." she wiped away her tears. "She was such a good girl..."

"Ok, well if you can think of anything, please call us." Derek said, handing her a contact card. "Again, really sorry for your loss."

Chapter 12

The Detectives walked away from the house, feeling troubled. Joe couldn't help but look uneasy as the lights flickered. The wind pushed against him as he climbed into his car. It pushed against the car, rocking it slightly from side to side. The power cables swung, and the tree branches swayed back and forth. The dried leaves on the ground circled and swirled as though it were dancing with the wind.

He started the car and headed back towards the station. "It's the end of the day now. I'll look through the files again before I go home. Maybe I will think of something that might help us get somewhere. At the moment, I feel like we are at a dead end."

"I know the feeling. It's like it is right there, but we can't seem to put my finger on what we are overlooking." Derek agreed.

They arrived at the station and swapped cars, ready to go home.

"I'll see you bright and early in the morning."

"All right. I'll see you around eight?"

"That's be perfect." Joe smiled.

"Let me know if you have a light bulb moment, won't you?"

"Yes, absolutely. As soon as I know what it is, or what to do."

Derek climbed into his car to drive away, and Joe went inside the station. The forensics took the victim's car to look for evidence of arsenic, already. He frowned and went and check on their progress.

Down at the lab, they scattered the dismantled car all over the floor.

"Did you find anything that could leak the arsenic?" he asked.

The mechanics shook their heads. "No sorry. The cars were actually in great condition. It doesn't appear to have been tampered with, or had any poisons put in the tank. It's clean. We are just about to put the cars back together before heading home."

Joe sighed. "Another dead end then, damn it."

He thanked the mechanics and went to look through the pictures of the crime scenes again. "Amy died at home, no sign of forced entry... Crystal died in the hospital... What the hell am I missing?"

Joe wondered if things could get any worse. He sighed and massaged his temples before combing his fingers through his curled hair. His eyes hurt and he felt nauseous, signs of an impending migraine emerging.

The lights flickered again. He went to his car and got ready to go home. "Maybe after a good night's sleep, the answer will come to me," he huffed. He shook his head, praying for a miracle.

He got home, and his wife greeted him at the living room door. "How was work?" she asked.

"Horrendous. It's another poisoning. I just can't work out how. Yet. I thought it might be from the car's air conditioner, but there is no sign that the cars were tampered with. So, I am guessing it is back to the drawing board... or..." he blinked, as though a light had suddenly blinked on. "Of course!"

"Light bulb moment?" she smiled.

He laughed and nodded. "I have only spoken to the people that like them. But what about the people that don't?"

"You can do that in the morning. Right now, you have a curry waiting in the microwave."

"Yes, but first, I need to give Detective Bells a call."

"Not until you have had your dinner," Megan repeated firmly.

Joe nodded in agreement and took his dinner out of the microwave and sat with it up the table to eat. His wife had already eaten, so was sitting in a chair watching her favourite music channel play. Half way through his dinner, his thoughts strayed to the victims. How many of the people who didn't like them wanted them dead? He worried, frowning as he chewed. The victims were usually well-liked, but some, he found in the past, were much more unpopular and that much harder to solve. The way the case was going, it was looking like it was going to be the latter—the nice girls that they were described to be may not be very nice at all. He swallowed his mouthful and sighed.

After Joe had finished his meal, he took his phone out of his pocket and called Derek. "Hey, you said to call as soon as I had a lightbulb moment."

"Yes, I did. I was just getting ready for bed. You need me to come and get you?"

"No, that's fine. We can do it tomorrow. I just wanted to update you. There was nothing on the cars. It came back clean. But, I was thinking, we have spoken to colleagues, family and friends. Maybe it is time to speak to the people that did not think they were so friendly."

"That sounds like a good next step. Shall we meet around eight, like we planned?"

"Yes. I will buy some coffee on the way down."

"What happened to not drinking coffee? Doctor gave you the all clear?"

Joe sighed, suddenly remembering his orders. "Oh... yeah. I guess I will have a decaf coffee then."

"Cheer up. I am sure you have got a little more time to wait. How many days has it been?"

"Almost a week, I think."

"Then you are halfway there. Keep it up. I will meet you outside your house at eight and then we can go straight to the station and find out who wasn't so nice to the victims."

"That sounds like a plan." Joe smiled.

"Good. I am going to go to bed now."

"Alright. Good night." Joe hung up the phone and turned to his wife. "He is going to bed. But I think we might actually get somewhere this time. One of them is bound to be the killer."

"That means that one of them is dangerous. Please, for the love of my sanity, please don't put yourself in harm's way."

"I will be careful," he replied, re-assuring her.

They went up the stairs and removed their clothes before climbing beneath their bed sheets.

The next morning, Joe woke up blinking. The temperature in the room was well below his usual comfortable 20 degrees. He shivered, then quickly grabbed his clothes from the wardrobe and drawers and pulled them on as fast as he could. Now wide awake, he went downstairs to put the heating on and then made himself a cup of decaf coffee. He opened the curtains in the lounge, revealing a still-dark street.

He made himself breakfast and watched as the seconds passed on his analogue clock hanging on the wall. He drained his cup with a last few big gulps and then went to get himself ready for the day.

He sighed, hoping that the enemy list would provide more answers than questions, and maybe even point toward the actual killer.

He put his bowl into the empty sink and poured himself another decaf coffee, itching to get started.

Joe poured the coffee into a thermal travel mug and headed to his car. He glanced down at his watch. It was just turning to fifteen minutes until eight o'clock, leaving him with plenty of time to get to the station.

At the station, the halls and offices were still and silent. The lights were not yet lit, and Joe was the first one to arrive. His footsteps echoed along the empty halls. He opened the door to his office and went inside. He went through the social media sites and started researching on who didn't like the victims. "Everyone writes everything on here. I am sure I will find statuses about the people they dislike..." he murmured.

After hours of scrolling, he finally came across a status that sounded less than happy. "Back stabbing bitches," he read. "That sounds promising." He opened the comments and printed a copy of the screenshot.

"This will do," Joe smiled. He put it in his pocket and went to make himself a drink. The staff room was still empty. He looked around, grinning. Finally, he opened the cupboard door and pulled out a cup, and then reached for a jar of coffee. He grabbed a teaspoon and dug out a big heap of the instant coffee before scooping it into the mug. Then, adding the two sugars and hot water, he went and sat down. He placed himself in the far corner, stirring the black liquid as he contemplated on what he needed to do next. He took a large mouthful of his full caffeinated coffee and smiled. The doors opened on the other side of the room and a light flickered on. "Joe?" It was Derek. "Why are you sitting in the dark?"

joe smiled, "Because no one was here."

"Alright. Why are you in a corner?"

"Coz I was being bad?" he replied meekly.

"Bad? What did you do?" he demanded. He walked over to his colleague and peered into his cup. "Ooh," Derek gasped. "seriously? Does your wife know?"

"Of course not! And you will not tell her. It is just one coffee. It will not do any harm."

"You, Joe, have a problem. Have you thought about going to AA meetings for addicts?"

"Meetings of coffee? Are you out of your mind? Don't be daft. I just need a caffeine hit to get me through the day. One cup will not do me any harm. Now, sit down and listen to my plan."

"Fine, but I am not covering for you if she finds out."

"You're supposed to be on my side, Derek," Joe insisted. He stood up, brushing himself off. The bits of carpet gripped the fibers of his white shirt, refusing to let go. He rolled his eyes before picking them off with his fingers.

"Yeah, but not against your doctor." His frown deepened. Joe looked tired, with heavy bags circling beneath his dark blue eyes. He seemed in desperate need of caffeine, but like most addicts, he couldn't stop at just one.

Joe grumbled but decided it was best not to mention it further. He finished his coffee and then pulled the printed screenshot out of his pocket. "This is a conversation I pulled earlier from social media. It looks like a few people really got into it a few weeks ago. It maybe nothing though."

"what was the argument about?"

"That's what I would like to know. It just says that someone was a backstabbing bitch. It could be about either of them. So, pour yourself a cup of coffee or something before we go."

"Alright. What about you? Are you having a decaf now that you are caffeinated?"

"No, I think I will just have a glass of ice water whilst I'm waiting. I need to drink some more water. It's not like I drink enough of it."

"So, you are taking something away from this, then?"

"Of course." Joe sighed. "I am not completely coffee reliant, you know."

"Once we have had our drink, we can find out the addresses of these people."

Derek nodded and took his laptop out of his bag before hanging it on his shoulder over his dark blue parker coat.

"You have a laptop? Since when?"

"Since today. I knew it might come in handy." He sighed. "I bought it a few weeks ago, but this is the first time I brought it out of my house. I am going to get a new one in a couple of months, so I think it is safe to come out with me."

"Alright. Check it out then. Hopefully, we can get some answers that would lead us to the killer, or at least to the murder weapon."

"Yeh, find the murder weapon, then we can find the killer," he agreed. "I'll log on now. You grab some water."

Joe made himself some water and sat back down. A few minutes passed in silence. Then, one by one, the rest of the police officers filed through into the building to start the day.

They left the station ten minutes later and climbed into the car outside. The sun was just peeking over the horizon. The light stretching out across the pavement in front of them, and shadows casting out over the houses and the parked cars. "Who is first on the list?" Derek asked.

"Lets start with the one who wrote the status. Coral Hoard. She lives a few miles down towards town. I'm very interested in hearing who and why someone was a bitch, and why she wrote it on Crystal's wall—and tagging Amy on there as well."

"So maybe she was calling them both backstabbers?" he frowned.

"That's the thought." Joe pulled in front of an old-looking house. Weeds had long taken over the garden, and the pavement was falling apart. "I think the weeds invaded a bit," Joe whispered.

"Seriously? I think the whole house may have been."

They got out of the car and raised his hand to knock on the door, hovering above the brass knocker. Joe waited for an answer.

Derek stared at the door, narrowing his eyes at it.

Joe rolled his eyes, then turned to his partner. "You can't knock with your mind. So, stop wasting time and knock on the door."

"Sorry. I was just thinking of what kind of person would let their house look so bad. It looks like the house was abandoned or something."

A young woman answered the door wearing a blue shirt and a white pair of jeans. She had long brown hair and brown ankle-high boots.

"Yes?" she asked, not bothering to ask who they were.

"I am Detective Bells and this is Detective Twit. We're from Homicide. I trust you know why we're here?"

"That's why I didn't ask for your name. I don't care. I asked you what you want—not for your autographs."

"We need to ask you some questions about the negative status you wrote on social media. Can you explain why you seem to call a couple of the women, names?"

"You mean, back stabbing bitches, right?"

Joe nodded. "Thats the one."

"Yeah. They slept with my boyfriend. He's not anymore though... We broke up."

"Ah. So you would be plenty happy about both Amy and Crystal's death then? Maybe slip them a little of poison?"

"Poison?" the woman gasped. "Not in a million years!"

"Why not?" Joe frowned. "You have motive."

"Yes, but for starters, I don't know a thing about plants. I wouldn't know how to get poison from a flower. I'd end up giving it to her in a damn vase and wait for the flower to grow legs or something."

"What about anyone else that didn't like her?"

"Fuck knows. Try going to the place she worked at. I am sure most of them don't get on too well."

"I am working on that. Who else had problems with them?" Joe demanded.

"Uh... I don't know. Like I said, go to her job. That is where she spent almost her entire year, anyway. If there is something not right, then it will be clear in her job."

They arrived back at the loan company. Joe sighed, "I have the oddest feeling that this place has something to do with those deaths..."

The phone rang. It was the hospital. Again.

"Yes, is there an update?" Joe asked.

"Of a sort. I have a call on hold from the next state over. They just had five people rushed in with the same symptoms. They're worrying about a pandemic."

"Which state?" Joe frowned.

"The one across the water."

Joe groaned, "Alright. I am on my way." He hung up the phone and then turned to Derek. "Another five people dead with the same symptoms. We gotta go to the next state over and find out what is going on there. Maybe we will get lucky."

Derek chuckled to himself. "Maybe the killer skipped states? It could be why we're at a dead end on this side?"

Chapter 13

J oe pondered on this comment with unease. "I really hope not. Our case is rather thin as it is." He combed his fingers through his hair as he struggled to think of his next move. People were dropping like flies, and they were running out of suspects. He pulled up his black trousers and bowed down, bending a knee to tie his laces. Anything to stall for time to give himself a few extra seconds. The people were giving him odd looks as they passed by. He straightened himself out, warily eyeing the dark grey clouds heading in their direction. He brushed himself down, glancing at the coffee shop on the corner.

Derek nodded. "I know. I'm just stating that this could be why we haven't found her yet."

"Well, let's look on this side of the water first before we travel to other states, shall we?"

"Alright fine. Where do you suppose we should go next?" Derek frowned, folding his arms, and stood rigid as he waited for the plan.

"I think we should go back and look at victims' houses." Joe added thoughtfully. "Just as soon as we know what we are looking for."

They went back to the workplace and searched all the rooms again, searching in draws and under tables and chairs. They raided cupboards and the toilets, making sure there was nothing left uncovered. "There has to be something that we are missing..." he repeated. He groaned to himself as he closed his eyes and tried to think more clearly. Interrupting his train of thought, or lack of, Joe's phone rang.

"Hello?" he answered.

"Yes, hello. We have a slight problem." It was the hospital. "What is the matter?"

"We just had another five people rushed in. All with the same symptoms."

"The same symptoms of poisoning? Are you certain?"

"Yes. It looks like they have been suffering for a while—three of them are dead on arrival."

"All right," Joe replied, looking flustered as the blood rushed to his face. "I am on my way now."

He turned to his colleague and grabbed a coffee from the side.

"I am going to need this. We have more victims. We are now looking at a serial killer." he stated, his expression suddenly looking worn and tired. "I have the feeling that this could just be the beginning of an actual nightmare."

"I hope not," Derek replied. "I want to go to sleep tonight. Not lay awake and wait for the phone to ring."

"You and me both," Joe replied. "I don't sleep a lot as it is. I really can't afford to have much less."

"Especially if you're not drinking coffee," Derek muttered.

Joe grunted his reply. "Yup, a complete nightmare."

The day was dragging on, but after an hour of driving, they finally reached the hospital. The nurses were waiting at the reception desk for them to arrive. "It's this way," the nurse stated, not wasting time greeting them.

"How many dead since we last spoke?" Joe asked.

"Four. The last one is in critical condition. But we can't do anything because we don't know how much poisoned they were given."

"As soon as we know which poison was used, we can have it tested and with any luck, find out how much and how long they were exposed to it." Joe replied. He ran his hand over his bald head in frustration. "All of my years as a detective, this is the first that we have anything like this..."

"I am sure that there will be others that'll make you cuss," Derek sighed.

They were led through a long hall with green walls and white marble flooring, and then went through a double door and shown to the victims' beds in a row. Four of them were covered with sheets, and the last was on a machine, wheezing.

"What are their names?" Derek whispered, feeling uncomfortable.

"Mark Stanely, Roger Mackle, Terry Newlook, and Kevin Card," she listed.

"They're not much older than their twenties either," Derek sighed.

The nurse shook her head. "Nope. They are all in their mid-twenties. "

"Ok. Can I have their addresses, please? Did you contact the parents yet?"

The nurse nodded. "Yes. They are on their way."

"Alright," Joe sighed. "I will wait here and get their addresses from the parents. Then maybe find out where they all worked and who had a problem with these people. Surely, they must have something in common, friends, a job, maybe a favourite pub?"

"You are welcome to wait. In the meantime, I will wait for the parents before I do the autopsy and then confirm that the poison is in their system."

"I think that is a good idea."

The two Detectives sat in the waiting room for the parents to arrive. The sun had set over the horizon, and the smell of freshly brewed coffee drifted through the halls from the cafeteria at the end of the corridor.

He cleared his throat, attempting to distract himself.

"How is you and your life at home?" Joe asked.

"Uh, it is not great to be fair," he grumbled, looking down at the floor. "Me and Silvia are having a few issues. But I am sure that we can work through it. After all, twenty-two years is hardly a number to be sniffed at, is it?"

"Married twenty-two years?" Joe gasped.

"What? No!" Derek said, slapping his forehead. "We've been to-gether for twenty-two years. We have been married for about twelve years. In fact, it will be our twelfth year in two months' time."

"That's great news," Joe smiled. "About how long you have been to-gether—not so great on the issues part, naturally."

"Thanks," he smiled sadly.

"What caused the issue?" Joe asked, prying. "If you don't mind me asking?"

"Oh, the usual. Not enough time at home, not enough attention... She had an affair. We're looking at what options we have."

"That sounds fair enough," Joe sighed. He opened his mouth to give some advice, but thought better of it and remained silent. No one likes a busybody.

The doors opened, and a line of parents walked through the door and up to the desk. "I am here about my kid," they said, one at a time.

"Over there," the nurse replied, pointing to the detectives.

"They will explain."

"Explain what?" a mother demanded, pulling the ponytail of her short blonde hair.

"Uh... We need you to come and sit in the rooms and we will come to you one at a time. The nurses will show you to your children whilst you are all waiting."

"OK then," the nurse agreed. She called them towards her and lead them down the same halls they had just came from not an hour ago. The first of the parents sat down with the detectives, tears streaming down their faces.

"I am so sorry for your loss," Joe sighed, speaking gently.

"What happened?" she demanded, tugging at her husband's arm.

"Your son was murdered." Joe explained, getting straight to the point. He was sick of having to keep breaking the news and decided that ripping the bandaid off was the best approach.

"Murdered? How?" she sobbed.

"Poison. It is likely they didn't even know what was going on. It would be like having the bug, and simply thought it would pass."

"Bug? What do you mean? I don't understand."

"Uh, bug like symptoms." Derek explained. "Again, I am really sorry."

"Was there anyone that he did not get on with?" Joe asked.

"Not really. He was kind enough. He wouldn't be mean. Sometimes, though, people irk him."

"Anyone in particular?"

"Not that I can think of, really. Just some difficult customers."

"Customers? Where did your son work?"

"Oh, you know- that loan place that has been so popular lately. What was it called?" she mumbled to herself, running the names through her head. "Oh, that was it. Loan Industries."

"You're kidding? Loan Industries was where he worked?"

"Yes. Why would I joke about that?" she snapped.

Derek lowered his head, suddenly remembering why they were having this conversation. "I am sorry. I did not mean to be insensitive. It was just a lightbulb moment. I have heard of this company quite a few times in the last couple of weeks. How long has he worked there for?"

"Not long. Only for the last six months. He really enjoyed helping people."

After they left the family home, they climbed into their car and sat in silence as the news sank in. "Too many people are dying, and they all work in the same place."

"I have noticed. I think it is time to go back to the company tonight and make sure we speak to everyone in charge. As soon as we have something to eat." Joe looked at the time on his watch. "Maybe tomorrow morning... we need to be well-rested. Go home and talk to your wife, sort things out. I just hope no one else dies in the meantime."

They headed home, and Joe walked through the front door of his house an hour later. His wife was sitting in front of the television with a cup of tea.

They were halfway through the night, watching their favourite show about wildlife, when the electric turned off.

"What now?" Joe grumbled. "As if my day wasn't bad enough?"

"It has been doing this for quite a while now. I am hoping the electricians would sort those cables out, so the wind doesn't keep knocking them loose." Megan commented, shrugging her shoulders.

She walked into the kitchen and emerged with a lighter. Finding her way through the dark, she lit the scented candles.

Joe blinked, as though the whole of his head had just switched on like a giant lightbulb. "Candles! Of course!" he gasped. "How the hell did I not see this before?" He grabbed his phone and immediately called his partner. "I know how it happened!" he blurted out, not waiting for a greeting.

"How what happened?" Derek asked. "I'm confused."

"The poisoning! I know how they got poisoned!"

"All right, tell me. How did it happen?"

"The candles!" Joe cheered. "It is in the candles. They have candles, but I don't know if it's the wax or the wick. I need to get to the Loan Industries, now. I need to know what they know about these candles."

Derek sighed, "Alright. I will be a few minutes. I literally just got into my pajamas, so I'll have to get changed again. In the meantime, call the company and let them know we are coming."

"Alright," Joe replied hastily. "Just don't doddle!"

Joe hung up the phone and went to grab his coat.

"Where are you going?" his wife asked.

"I am heading over to the Loan Industries company. I think I have finally got a lead on this damn case!"

She sighed and gave him a kiss and a hug before returning to her own candles. She walked to the bookshelf and picked up a book with a shiny cover. It was a romance book, with silhouette shadows of a couple standing in front of a full moon. A book, he noticed, that she had read dozens of times. The pages were falling out, and the cover was bent and worn along the spine.

He walked out the front door, holding the phone to his ear as he waited for Loan Industries to answer his call. After the seventh ring, there was finally a reply.

"Bout time!" Joe huffed.

"I'm sorry, who's this? I'm just about to leave for the day."

"Sorry, it's Detective Twit from Homicide. You need to stay there a little longer. I am on my way and have a couple of questions," Joe replied. "I'm with my partner, Detective Bells. You remember us, right?"

"Alright. I won't be waiting long, though. Are you nearby?"

"I'm literally five minutes away. I have an idea that might explain why your employees are turning up dead."

"Ok. I will stay for a few minutes then. But any later than twenty minutes, my wife will look to kill me as well." Mr Handler replied. "I will see you soon."

Joe hung up the phone and drove towards the tall building. The floors towered above them like a giant glass tower. He pulled to the side and noticed the manager standing by the doors with a scarf and coat fastened. His hands buried deep into his pockets, trying to keep himself warm from the bitter, frosty night air.

"Make this quick," Handler said, greeting the Detectives. He stepped aside, allowing the Detectives into the building, just as the last of the employees were leaving their shift.

"Ok. There are several people being killed off, and they all work in your company. So, what is different? Surely something out of the ordinary had happened over the last past month."

"Uh, not much to be fair." he replied, frowning. He looked around, deep in thought, as he tried to confront the stars for answers. "Oh, there was one about five weeks ago." He remembered. "There was a little present on the desk. Everyone in the building got one. I'm assuming that someone was leaving a Christmas present for us all. It was a delightful surprise. Just a little box."

"Did you open it?" Joe frowned.

Carl nodded. "Of course I did. Such a nice little box. Why wouldn't I?"

"What was it?" Joe asked, though he already knew the answer. He needed confirmation without having words put there for him.

"It was a scented candle."

Joe blinked. There it was, the connection between all the victims who had died. The murder weapon. "And you say everyone in the building got one?"

Johnathan nodded again, "It smells like fruit." he smiled. "Strawberry and Vanilla I believe."

"Uh, how many people work in this building and got this thoughtful gift?" Joe asked. He turned his back, hearing footsteps behind him. It was Detective Bells, finally catching up.

"What did I miss?"

"Nothing much. The Detective was just asking me about the candles. It is a lovely gift."

"Yes, how long have you used it for?" Joe asked, stepping back cautiously.

"Only the once. Thankfully, I have been sleeping early, so I hadn't needed to use them yet. I like my candles, but they don't last me very long."

"Ok. I am going to need everyone's number and address and their names..." Joe said carefully, trying not to panic. "I know we are in the middle of another power cut, but time is of the essence. Those candles are probably the murder weapon." he explained. "Do not light them until I am certain whether they're dangerous."

THE LAST GIFT 65

"What are you talking about? Fire is dangerous. That is why we do not leave candles unattended."

"Exactly. Which is why the killer may have put the poison into it."

He turned to Derek and tried to speak as slow as he could, his tone becoming tense. "I need you to go to the victims' houses and collect all the candles. We don't know which one is the one they got from the work."

"It will be the jar ones," Carl replied casually. He fastened his leather coat, clutching the seams nervously. "They all came with lids."

"That might help." He blinked, thanking Johnathan as he turned back to his colleague. "Collect all the ones that have a jar, but collect those without as well, in case the killer was not picky about the type of candle was being used."

Derek nodded and immediately went on his way.

Joe massaged his temples. Another migraine was emerging, and this time he had no coffee to calm his nerves. He took a deep breath and tried to sound calm. "Just how many people work in your company in this building?" he asked, hoping for a small number.

"Only about three hundred people," he replied.

Joe swallowed hard. "Three hundred people. Is... That a small number is it?" he squeaked. He held his neck, pinching the opening of his airways as he tried to breathe. "I really hope that I am wrong..." he said. "Otherwise, that is three hundred people looking at a death sentence."

"A what now? You still haven't told me what is going on?" Johnathan asked.

"Oh, sorry. Those candles might be laced with arsenic. Which is why your employees are dropping like flies. They all think they have the bug, and then they get worse and die. It is a nasty way to go. But who could be that angry?"

"Uh... Bug?" he stammered. He swallowed hard, looking uneasy. "I had a call from a few people yesterday about them being sick with the bug, a real nasty one, they said."

"Was this around yesterday evening?" Joe asked.

Johnathan nodded, "Yes. Five of them."

"Sorry dude. They died last night at the hospital."

"All five of them?"

Joe sighed, looking miserable. "Four of them. The fifth is in critical condition."

Johnathan groaned. "Who could be so cruel? I'm not a great guy, but even this is beyond what I am capable of."

Chapter 14

Joe's phone rang. He answered the phone and held it to his ear. Worry clutched at his gut, twisting it into a cold hard knot.

"What's the news?" he asked, noticing the caller was Derek.

"Confirmation," he said.

"So the candles is killing them?" He thought for a minute. This was terrible news. "Which part of the candle?"

"It is on the wooden wick. The candle wicks were soaked in arsenic before the killer stuck it in the wax."

"That's cold," Joe grumbled. He told Derek to return to the Loan Industries, and then they would have to contact all the employees at the building to send the candles they had got from there to them. "Three hundred candles, and we don't know how many of them have been lit..." Joe gasped, leaning back against the wall. "The death count would be a disaster."

"My business would be in ruins! I would have to train new workers on how to do this job. I could lose so much money!"

"I would be more concerned about your life," Joe frowned. "You used the candle too. I would suggest going to the hospital immediately for a checkup. Who knows how much you have been exposed?"

"Are you serious?"

"You heard what the candles do, right?" Joe explained. He had no patience for people that only think of themselves.

"Alright fine. I will go home and get that candle now."

"I would. You said your wife is at home. You wouldn't know if she uses the candles too, would you?" Joe asked, frowning. He ran his hands over his head, trembling. It wouldn't just be the workers that would die, but their families, too. Including children.

"Oh, good lord!" Carl gasped. "My wife! My kids!" he screamed. "They all might be dead!"

"Get the candle, blow it out, and get yourself and your family to the hospital as quickly as you can. Don't waste time, just do it."

Carl nodded, running to his car. Then out like a shot, his tires screamed down the road as he headed home, and hopefully not towards a fatal accident.

Joe headed towards the hospital to give them the news. The waiting room already filling quickly with other incidents such as fights and accidents. Some of them were sick or hurt. He sighed. If they get rushed from the poisoning, the hospital was about to become very hostile. He held his breath and looked at his partner. "We need to make sure none of those candles get lit."

"Only way to do that is to secure those power lines," Derek said. "I don't think we qualify as electricians. Other than that, we need to get an email out to all the employees here to give us their candles and not to light it. But make sure that it is the ones they got from Loan Industries and not to send us the wrong ones."

"Let's just hope that we are not too late." Joe sighed. They headed back to the station and went straight for the computer and on to the email page.

They wrote emails and send them to all the contacts they had. "Please don't be too late," Joe mumbled.

Once all the directions were passed around, they added a note to the bottom. "Emergency Meeting in the morning at nine o'clock in the waiting area."

"Do you think they will turn up?" Derek frowned.

"We need to make sure that they get checked over. I am going to call the medical examiner, and hopefully, she will assist us tomorrow at the meeting. Check them there and then, so if they're exposed, take them directly to the hospital to be sorted."

"Alright. Then there is nothing more we can do. It is time to go home and rest. We need to be here early enough so that everything is ready- and hope we don't get a stampede of poisoned employees."

Joe's phone rang. He answered it, immediately feeling the wave of dread. "Detective, I just had the family in for check up that you sent. They are OK, only a minor exposure. As long as there are no more poisonous candles in their house, they should make a full recovery."

"Thank goodness," Joe sighed, relieved. "Now we just need to find out who was doing this to them."

"Yeah, and why? I hardly doubt someone woke up one day and thought, you know what—lets kill a ton of people and then maybe have a cup of tea. Someone got pissed off, and not over something small. It would need to be an ongoing thing that had been going on for a long while. But who?"

"Once we have the candles from everyone, we can find out. Surely someone knows who the presents had come from?"

"I hope so. Otherwise, we will have to look at unhappy customers and disgruntled employees over the last six months. It could take several weeks to get to them all."

"Yes, and by then, it might be too late for any of them." Joe stated sadly.

"At least we now know what is causing the deaths, and how. We just need to get all the candles back for evidence, and then get the who. Piece of cake," Derek smiled. "We will have this wrapped up in no time."

"The perfect line for those famous last words situations," Joe grumbled.

"What do you mean?" he frowned. "Last words?"

"You heard the saying. I know you have. Now, I just hope that they all get the email and not use the candles."

"We won't know for sure until tomorrow."

"I know that. Now, time to go home and get some sleep."

They headed home and worried about what the next day would bring them.

The following day, Joe woke up feeling a deep sense of dread. He sat up and slowly got out of his bed, being careful not to wake his wife, who was still sleeping next to him. He had his breakfast and got ready to start his day. Despite having restrictions on his caffeine intake, he switched on the kettle and have one, anyway. "I need this," he whispered to himself. It still tied his gut in a knot, anticipating the fallout from seeing how many people were affected and exposed by the poisonous candles.

He poured his coffee into his favourite mug and sat down at the table in silence.

Half an hour later, footsteps descended the stairs and echoed along the hall. "Couldn't sleep?" his wife asked.

He shook his head. "No. Those candles are a nightmare. It isn't just the workers that were getting poisoned, but children and wives were too. Can you imagine what kind of monster would risk endangering children's lives? It's unthinkable..."

"Perhaps the killer simply didn't take the others into consideration," she assured him.

"It still seems monstrous," he huffed. "And that doesn't excuse sending out hundreds of poisoned candles to people. All of those people are going to die. The hospitals and the morgue are going to be horrific, and then there are the funeral directors that are going to be rushed off their feet."

"And they are going to make a lot of money from the extra work," Megan smiled. "So maybe the motive is more money related?"

Joe looked at her with a smile. "Perhaps. But then why poison the entire building?"

He finished his coffee, hoping his wife didn't realise that it was fully caffeinated and not the decaf edition, and went to get ready to go to work.

When he arrived at the station, Derek was there waiting for him, smoking a cigarette by the entrance.

"I didn't know you smoked," Joe frowned, looking less than impressed.

"I quit, but this case has me on edge," he replied defensively.

"Ah. Same reason I am still hitting the caffeine then." He looked around, thinking about what to do next. "We need to speak to the employees at Loan Industries. Come on," Joe sighed.

When they arrived at the building, there was already a growing crowd waiting for them to turn up. Some workers cheered, others grumbled, though a few looked on with disinterest and boredom.

"Thank you for coming today. I am sure that you have a lot of questions. But my first question is, have you all brought your candles with you?"

"Yes, but why?" someone called out.

Joe narrowed his eyes as he searched the crowd for who spoke. All he could tell was that it was a middle-aged man. "Who was that, please?"

"My name is Aaron Quickby. Why are we bringing in our present?"

"Because it was laced with poison." Derek replied. The crowd talked in hushed tones, worriedly.

"Therefore, we asked you to bring it in as soon as possible and not to light it."

"What if we had already used it?" Aaron asked, wearing a black suit with a white polka-dot tie. He had blonde hair and bright blue eyes.

"Then if you felt unwell, with bug like symptoms, I would suggest going to the hospital. They will deal with you there and check you over for exposure. It might be the candle or the bug. Which is why it is important to get checked. You would have to use the candle for quite a while for it to make you feel unwell."

"How long?"

"About half of the candle, at least."

More murmurs travelled around the room like a game of Chinese Whispers. "Are we going to die?"

"As long as you get checked out and stop using the candle, you will be fine. If you continue to use the candle, though, you would continue exposure to the poison in it."

"So we will be OK?" another called out. It was a woman this time with long wavy red hair wearing a long black dress and black heels.

"Yes, you will be fine. But if you are feeling unwell, please come and speak to my associate, Sian. She will look you over here and let you know if you need the hospital trip or simply a good night's sleep."

Joe cleared his throat. "On another note, can someone please tell me why somebody is trying to kill you all"?

"You mean it was on purpose?" Aaron gasped, horrified.

This time the room fell silent, as guilty looking faces washed across the room like a wave. "Oh dear, I can see that many of you know why this is happening. Would you like to share with the class?"

"I, uh, I think it is because we are not the nicest of people. But our job isn't to be nice. It is to be ruthless and make sure the job gets done and that they paid the loans."

"You have something specific in mind?" Derek prompted. "It was a bit of a vague answer. We will need a little more information."

"There is this woman. She is called Adelia. She used to work here."

"This woman, Adelia. What can you tell me about her?" Joe asked.

"Well.... It is hard to say. We made her quit."

"You made her quit? What? All of you?" Joe frowned. "That wasn't very nice. What did she do to you?"

"Made us work harder and longer hours." someone called out. A small man with a pair of jeans and a white shirt stepped forward.

"Yeah," a woman sighed. "But we got paid more money, and we weren't working for peanuts. She made sure of that."

"So, what was the problem?" Joe asked again. "Why force her to quit when she was making you money?"

"She knew stuff. That's all. There was no privacy. We look into our customers, not into each other's lives. Some of us aren't angels, and wanted our lives to stay private."

"So you made her quit. Did she at least get to keep her home? What made her so mad? Just losing her job?"

The guilty expressions turned into remorse. "We may have done a little more than that."

"Explain, please?" Derek demanded, already disliking the company and the workers.

"We sent her across state, so that she wouldn't even be in the same area or postcode as us. We pushed her right out across the water."

"You lost her job and chased her out of her home?!" he gasped. "And you wonder why she's pissed?"

"It wasn't just us!" Aaron argued. "The boss did it as well. He didn't want to pay her, so he tried to have her shipped away. Those workers across the sea went further than we did."

"I will not like this, am I?" Joe sighed again. His migraine returning.

"They tried to have her killed." Aaron said. His tone was flat and emotionless, as though he were reading from a script.

"You know this for a fact?"

"Yeh. I am friends with some workers across the water."

Aaron grumbled.

Derek pinched the end of his nose as he tried to put things into perspective. "So, this is why she's trying to kill you all, then? Revenge," he stated.

They all nodded, confirming their guilt.

"Well, isn't this interesting? Instead of finding a motive for each one of you, she has a single motive for all of you."

"Well, let's hope we can find her before someone else pisses her off and tries to send her across the continent for helping."

Derek shook his head, "I would hate to imagine how you would all react if she was nasty as you had been to her."

Joe tried to think things through as he searched the faces for something more. "Who can tell me which building she was working at?"

"It is the building that used to be a candle making factory," Aaron replied, not missing a beat. "She cleared it out before she quit."

"You mean before you made her quit?"

"Yes, we admit, we're horrid. Now, what can we do?" Aaron snapped irritably.

"You can try to not piss anyone else off," Joe sighed.

Chapter 15

Detectives Joe Twit and Derek Bells took the ship over to the next state.

The buildings across the water loomed over the horizon with sky scrapers and tower blocks. The clouds hung over them with heavy humidity, causing Joe and Derek to sweat.

"The humidity in here is suffocating me," Derek complained. "Isn't there any air?"

"I know. It isn't great. But hopefully we won't be here long. We just need to find the Loan Industries in this region and see who else had pissed Adelia off." He looked around to find a sign that would lead them in the right direction. "They said it used to be a candle making place. So, I am assuming there would be something around here that would point us the right way..."

Other than a few signs signaling shops and paid parking, the signs were few; none of which was helping them.

"This is madness!" Joe ranted. He collected his car from the harbour and then decided it was time to use his SatNav.

He turned left into a narrow street, slowing down his pace for the sharp and very blind corner. A silver landrover car greeted him near the top of the road, rushing down the narrow path. Joe slowed to a stop, tucking himself into the curb as far as he could. A parked car in front of him, almost on top of the corner, stopped him from tucking in completely against the curb. The car approached him, beeping as it passed, missing him by a hair! "Therefore, the cars aren't supposed to be parked on the corner!" Joe growled, gritting his teeth. "How the hell are we supposed to see each other coming in time to move out of the way?!"

he banged his fists against the steering wheel, then took a deep breath before continuing down the road.

"Dude, you need to calm down. You're getting road rage," Derek huffed.

Joe looked at him, scowling furiously. "Would you be telling me to calm down if we were hit? I doubt it. Some of these drivers are border-lining on reckless endangerment."

After they finally arrived, they headed inside the building. Some-one covered the large machines with a blanket at the back. In the front was a small desk and a row of computers. Joe frowned. "They're turning the candle factory into an office?"

"I know. It makes little sense, does it?" Derek laughed.

He looked around and saw a shadow in a doorway at the end of the large, dusty room.

"Excuse me!" Joe called out, following Derek's gaze.

"How can I help you?" the shadow replied.

They showed him their police detective badges and walked up to the silhouetted figure. As they approached it, the figure slowly turned into a man smoking a cigarette, leaning against the doorway.

"Yes. What can you tell me about Adelia, please?" Joe asked.

"Ah yes. Her death is no surprise. Are you here to collect her things? She left nothing. She quit shortly after she began working over here. I guess she couldn't handle the stress."

"What makes you think she is dead?" Joe frowned, the tone in his voice slightly elevated to a confused tone.

"Well, you are detectives asking for Adelia. I just assumed..." he stammered, suddenly looking guilty and sheepish. "Oops," he com-mented, trying to shrug off his mistake.

"I am from homicide, but her death isn't what I am here for. Should I be looking into her death then, assuming you know something I don't?"

"Uh, well, if it isn't her death you are looking at, then who are you investigating for being dead?"

"You mean, who died?" Derek scoffed. "Are you serious?"

"Yeah, that's the question. Both. Who died, and are you being serious?"

"Many people died in your company. So why should I be looking for Adelia's body as well?"

"Uh, I would recommend speaking to my boss. I dont know anything!"

He turned and raced out of the building, slamming the door behind him.

"That was odd."

"Very. What do you think he's running from?" Derek frowned, scratching his head.

"From that reaction? I would probably say that we are looking for another body."

"Well, if Adelia isn't the killer, who the hell is?" Derek grumbled. "I thought we were on to something."

"So did I. Maybe we are onto something else instead, which is just as important." He sighed, looking around at the building. "We better start looking for clues. I'll call forensics and get them down here to process the place. It looks like it is going to be a big job."

"I agree. Maybe we can stop for something to eat when they get here. I am starving!"

Joe shook his head. He was hungry as well, but food was the last thing on his mind. People were dying, and he needed to know why and who was causing these deaths.

Once the forensics arrived, they looked around the building for some clues. The room was covered with dust; the floor had been swept but not mopped. He could see the brush strokes of the broom going from one side of the room to the next. He uncovered the machinery, which only puzzled him more. "That is very odd. These machines are clean. I am sure the sheets wouldn't protect them from all the dust, right?"

Derek shrugged. "I wouldn't have a clue. Maybe that was what it was supposed to do?"

Joe looked around the room, looking for an explanation. "Perhaps," he murmured to himself. "Or perhaps these machines were used to make those candles recently."

"That would make sense, making the deadly candles before covering them up again. We could check them for fingerprints." Derek cheered.

"Yes, they should." Joe called over to one of the men in blue suits and walked over. "Hi, I'm Detective Twit. These machines need to be dusted for fingerprints as well. These could be what made the murder weapon and could give us a clue about who has been behind on all these deaths."

The man in blue nodded, and went over to his men, signalling to get to work. Two men grumbled and made their way over to a large oven.

Satisfied the machines would be inspected, Joe looked at his watch. "Come on, Derek. Let's get something to eat."

"Great idea. Where are we going?"

"I'm thinking of chicken curry..." he smiled. "I hope they have one nearby."

"They should. This place is a city, right? What city doesn't have a curry house?"

The hospital was quiet. Only three people were waiting inside the waiting room, hoping to be seen. One man was wearing rags and had a broken leg. Another was a woman, clutching her arm. The receptionist sighed and noticed a younger woman with a head injury. The blood was still trickling down her face.

A nurse exited from a small office and called out a name.

"Julia Edwards?" she called out.

The young woman got up and staggered over to the nurse with a lopsided smile. "Hello nurse, thank you for seeing me."

"So, what happened here?" she asked softly.

"I feel off my chair trying to replace a light bulb. I wouldn't recommend doing it alone. Dangerous work," she joked. She winced, leaning back so that the nurse wouldn't touch it.

"I bet it is feeling a little sore," the nurse chuckled gently, trying to relax her patient.

"Just a little."

"Can I see?" she asked.

The young woman nodded and closed her eyes. With the slightest touch of the nurse's fingertips, the young woman flinched. "Ow!"

"Oh yes," the nurse stated. "You are going to need stitches. But you will be fine."

The young woman thanked her and slouched back in her chair.

"So I can go home?"

"Hm, I wouldn't recommend it just yet. It is a head injury. How long ago was this?"

"About four hours ago," she replied, checking her watch.

"Have you got anyone who can be with you for the next 24 hours"?

"No, I am on my own."

The nurse frowned, then smiled gently. "You can stay here for the next 24 hours, just to be on the safe side. Then you can go home tomorrow. Are you feeling alright, other than sore? No nausea or what-have-you?"

Julia shrugged. "I am alright. I am just feeling a little tired. It has been a long day and I don't sleep very well at the moment."

"Alright. You can take a nap as soon as we get you a bed."

The nurse called over her colleague and spoke to her in soft tones. After a brief discussion, glancing back at the young woman with long blonde hair. She nodded. "My colleague Colleen will take you to a room to get some rest."

Julia thanked them and stood up, still shaking.

"Let's get those stitches and get you to bed," Colleen commented, tightening her bright red hair into a ponytail.

The nurse sighed and called out to the next patient to be seen.

Nurse Darcy looked around at the reception desk, suddenly hearing worried whispers from the queue.

"What's going on?" Darcy frowned.

"We're about to get rushed," Colleen replied in hushed tones. She peered around the corner to the line, counting how many people had just arrived. "Looks like about twenty people. And they all look like hell. We might be in for a long day and night."

"Oh, hell," she grumbled. "Did someone break a mirror?"

Julia dealt with the broken leg and the sprained arm, and sent them to the next doctor to get a sling and a cast. She sighed. Now it was time to deal with the new patients. "Robin Colon!" she called, opening the door. "How can I help you today?"

"I don't feel very well," he groaned. He hunched over a cardboard sick bowl, moaning. "And I think I saw blood in my pee. And I keep having stomach cramps and really watery... er.. stools."

"Ah, alright. Anything else?" she asked, already feeling concerned. "Yeah, is it normal for my hair to be falling out"?

Darcy cleared her throat and went over to her colleague. Colleen was back from taking Julia to her bed. "I think we have another one of those poisoned victims. If these all have the same, we have a serious problem."

"How many of you work for Loan Industries?" Colleen called out.

Eighteen of them raised their hands.

"How many of you received a new candle and had been using it?"

They kept their hands raised. Colleen turned to Darcy, keeping her voice calm. "You need to take them all to the next ward. It is empty, they can be dealt with there. I'll call for backup to deal with them when they arrive."

Darcy nodded, swallowing back a hard lump in her throat.

"What about you other two?" Darcy asked, trying to smile. "What is the matter?"

"I don't work for Loan Industries, but I got a candle from my son." he smiled. "Is this serious?"

"Follow the others to the ward," Darcy directed calmly.

She turned to the last patient, a woman with a young baby. "We had a candle too. My husband got one from work. What is going on?"

"Alright. Please follow the others, and you'll be treated there with the rest."

"Why are we going to another ward?" the woman demanded.

"Miss..."

"Kathy," she interrupted. "My name is Kathy, and this baby is called Doreen. She is six months old. She is my daughter and is only six months old. Please, tell me what is going on?"

"It's probably just a bug. We'll give you all a checkup in the other ward. Try to relax and stay calm. Alright?"

Dorreen raised an eyebrow, not believing the words from the nurse's mouth. "A bug?"

"Probably. But the right people will check you over when you get there."

"Alright," Doreen sighed, defeated. "Please, check on my daughter first. I am concerned... she isn't looking very well."

Darcy signalled to Colleen and spoke to her. "Please check on the kid and take them to the others. These all dealt with the candles too," she whispered.

"Alright. Follow me," Colleen instructed. "We'll find out why you're feeling poorly."

Once the last of the patients left, she slouched back in her chair and took a deep breath. Then, pulling herself together, picked up the phone receiver and called Joe for an update. She prayed for the strength to find the words to tell him, but all she could think about was what would happen to those people and cried.

A young man raced into the hospital, his trousers and shirt disgruntled and his shoes muddied from the muddy puddles. He had spiky black hair and a nose stud, and a chain link for a belt hanging on his jeans. He panted, gasping for breath as he finally reached the reception desk. "Hi, I had a call to say that my wife was here? Is she alright? What about my little girl? Is Doreen alright?"

"Calm down please, I need their full names," the receptionist sighed. She glanced at the clock in front of the room, hanging behind the patient lines. It was almost ten o'clock at night.

"Sorry, my little girl is Doreen. She is six months old, and my wife is Kathy Wilson. Please, they came in earlier. I couldn't get off work any sooner."

"And your name?" she asked him.

"My name is Thomas Wilson."

She typed the information on her computer and took a deep breath. "Alright. They are down the hall. I will just call someone to come and get you so that they can speak to you about their condition."

"Condition?" he frowned. "Are they alright?"

She took another deep breath. "They were very ill when they came in, as were a lot of others. You may need a checkup as well," she hinted.

He gave her a hard stare, pressing his lips together tightly. "What the heck are you talking about?"

She grabbed the phone and called Coreen to the front of the desk. "This is Thomas Wilson. He is the husband and father of Kathy Wilson and the baby, Doreen Wilson- they came in earlier during the rush. What is the news?"

Coreen's face paled, but her expression remained unchanged as she stared blankly at her colleague. "As expected," she replied briefly.

"What the hell does that mean?!" Thomas demanded, growing more agitated by the minute, becoming worried and scared. "Tell me!"

Coreen took Thomas to an empty room and took a deep breath. "You need to sit down," she told him. "The news is going to be a hard one to swallow."

Thomas sat down, pulling his chain to one side so that he wouldn't be sitting on it. He looked at the nurse's grim expression as she struggled to find the words. "It's really bad," she began. "There were many people who had the same problem, and I will have to have words with the families. Do you recall getting a candle from your company, Loan Industries?" she asked.

He shrugged casually. "Of course. It was a present, though I am not entirely sure... what has this got to do with my family?"

"The candles—it was laced with poison." Colleen explained, as calm as she could. She sat herself down, feeling herself tremble and shake inside. "Every person in the company- in two states that we know of, has had this same present, and had become very unwell."

"So, the candles are making people sick? Who would do that? Is my family sick?"

"Please, I am getting to it... Sorry... everyone that has been using the candle has been getting really sick."

"You said that. Someone is using candles to make people sick," he repeated in a huff.

"It was making them sick, but it wasn't there to make them sick. Someone had laced the candles with poison." She looked at him and waited for the penny to drop.

"So, they are very sick. And will need some treatment to get better, right?" Thomas replied, though his expression changed to despair. "Right?"

"Uh. Anyone that has used the candles so far, had died..." she replied sadly. "Th- that includes..."

"No!" Thomas exclaimed angrily. "Don't you dare say it!"

"The police are involved. The candles have, so far, been sent over two states, and people have been dropping like flies. They're trying to find out who did this."

"Two states? And they're all...? I want to see them." he stuttered, pleading. "I want to see my baby girl, and I want to see my wife. Where are they?"

"I can take you to them, but I must warn you—they're... gone."

"Don't tell me that!" he screamed, grabbing the mug off the table and launched it against the room, watching as the cup hurtled towards the wall and smashed into dozens of pieces. "They are not... They're not!"

Coreen took a deep, shaky breath, and lead Thomas to the end of the hall and into the ward where the candle victims had been placed. Rows of beds lined up, stretching from one side to the room to the next. Each bed had someone in it, covered head to toe with a white sheet.

At the far end of the hall was a bed with two occupants, with a larger sheet covering them both.

Thomas stood on the bed, shaking violently before collapsing to his knees and sobbed. "Who—I will find out who did this," he whispered. "And then, I am going to commit a murder that psychopaths can only dream of. The devil himself would shake."

Chapter 16

Detective Joe Twit got off the phone and slipped the iPhone into his pocket. His face was pale and sullen. He cleared his throat before turning to his partner. "That was the hospital," he reported. "There were more deaths."

"How many?" Derek asked, his brow creases deepened as he braced himself for the worst.

"Twenty. Twenty deaths, all with the same symptoms."

"Scented candles."

"Yeah. What's the body count now?" he frowned, counting the victims in his head. "Must be almost thirty now. Shit. Shit, shit, shit, shit!" He turned around and kicked the wall, wincing. "Dammit!"

"We need you to keep your head on, not lose your sanity. We should go up to the hospital and talk to the medical examiners. Find out how long they have been exposed," Derek told him, as calmly as he could. He took a deep breath, his insides shook, and the nausea turned his stomach. "We have got to find out who has been doing this- and find out what has happened to Adelia. She is the murderer, or she is the victim. We have to find her. I think she is the key behind all this either way."

Joe sighed, "You are right. She is. We had better go to the hospital and find out where she lives, and then speak to the families. She must have confided in somebody, right?"

Derek nodded. "I'll get the car."

They climbed into the car a few minutes later and headed back down to the hospital. It seemed with this case; they were down there more often than the station. "Someone has a lot of explaining to do," Joe grumbled.

As they arrived at the hospital, the nurses took them straight over to the ward where the bodies were waiting. "Thank goodness that you are here," Coreen said, greeting them enthusiastically.

"What happened?" Derek asked.

"We had the husband come in, after hearing his wife and baby were admitted with the same symptoms as the others."

"Oh, was it that bad?" Joe asked.

"Worse. Megan and the baby died shortly after arriving. The baby died first. The mother watched her baby die... it was the last thing she saw before dying herself. It was horrible, and then the husband arrived and had to be told about their deaths."

"Shit. That is bad. He didn't take it very well, I'm guessing." Joe stated.

"No, he took it badly." Coreen said, confirming the worst. "Joe, the baby was only six months old."

Joe blinked, a wave of dread, and despair washed over him. He dragged his hands down his face, trying to keep himself in check.

"Poor bloke. Alright, I'm going to need his name and address. I'll track him down and talk to him."

They left the building with hunched shoulders and migraines. "Haven't you got a doctor appointment today? To review your blood pressure levels?"

"Oh yeah," he groaned. "I just hope that my levels are low enough that I can go back to drinking coffee without feeling guilty."

"You check your blood pressure. I'll hunt down the families so we can visit them after you're done."

Joe nodded, "Alright. I will see you soon." He took out his phone and called for a taxi. He had to find his way back across the water and get his car before heading out towards the doctors for his checkup. "Please, let me have this. I really need a large coffee after today."

Joe and his wife arrived at the doctors' surgery and sat down in the waiting room. "You think that you'll have your blood pressure lower?" she asked him.

He shrugged, "I don't know. I hope so. I really want to drink coffee." He looked around the room, noting about ten people waiting in front of him. Most of them looked like they had a cold. They were called in for the checkup. He stood up and nervously made his way to the office. The doctor stood in the doorway and then offered him a seat.

"How has 'no caffeine' been treating you?" the doctor asked.

Joe shrugged. "Isn't that what you are going to tell me? I have been irritable and twitchy and very stressed. How do you think it has been treating me?"

The doctor cleared his throat and took out the blood pressure meter, and wrapped the cloth around his arm. "Let's see if you can start drinking coffee again..." he stated, thinking out loud.

"I hope so. It has been a very stressful week." Joe grumbled.

After a few minutes of the doctor checking results and writing notes onto the computer, he put his pen down and looked at Joe who was sitting on the edge of his seat. "Good news. It is lower than the last visit. I was hoping it would improve a little more, but for the moment, you can start drinking coffee again. But..."

"But?" Joe frowned. "I don't like the sound of that."

"Hardly anyone does. But yes, there is a but. But you are limited to drinking only four cups of coffee a day. I want you to come back in two weeks, and we will look at your blood pressure again. Understood?"

Joe sighed and nodded. It wasn't the result he wanted, but at least he could finally drink coffee without feeling guilty.

"Thank you, doctor. I will see you in two weeks, then."

Joe walked out of the office and grabbed the money from his pocket. His wife frowned. "What are you doing?" she demanded.

"What do you think I am doing? I may drink coffee now. So, I am going to get some coffee."

"Already?" she frowned. "You're going to go straight into it?"

Joe sighed. "Do you want to know what my day has been like already so far?"

She nodded. "It can't be that bad."

"I got a call from the hospital," he explained. "Twenty dead, including a mother and a six-month-old baby. All because of those damn candles."

"Ooh. That is rough. OK, have a small coffee; just don't overdo it." She replied, devotedly.

He walked towards the closest cafe across the road and went over straight to the front desk. "Can I order two coffees, please?"

She frowned again. "I said don't overdo it, and you order two?"

He shook his head. "You amaze me sometimes. They are not both for me. One of them is for you."

"Oh, thanks. Sorry," she mumbled.

"You want a coffee, yeah?" he asked.

"Yes, please."

He sighed and turned his attention back to the waiter at the front of the desk. "Yes, the two coffees please." he gave the waiter the money and went to sit down. "I'll have the coffee with you, drop you off home, and then I have to get back to work."

"Alright. I hope you find out who is doing this," she said sadly.

"So do I. I just hope the killer makes no more candles."

They finished their coffees in silence, and then Joe stood up and then went to take his wife home.

"Megan, you know I love you, right?" Joe called out, watching her fish her keys out of her handbag. She wiped her feet on the pink doormat and looked back at him. She pulled out her keys and smiled. "Yes, of course I do," she replied. She pulled out the elastic band from her hair, releasing her long black hair from its restraints, falling to halfway down her back.

He sighed and took a deep breath. Though he could still see her through the gap between the curtains. He smiled. She was wearing the pink shirt and dark blue skinny jeans that he had bought for her before the case started. He cleared his throat and pulled away from the curb, and turned his attention to the case at hand.

Joe arrived at the police station and went to pour himself a cup of coffee. Whilst he was pouring the liquid into the mug, he heard footsteps approaching from behind him.

"I take it that the doctor gave you the all clear?" Derek asked, smiling.

"For now. I have to have another check up again in two weeks. Have you tracked down the addresses of the families?"

"Yes, they are a bit all over the place. I have told them we will come and see them all today and ask a few questions."

Joe nodded, patting Derek on the back. "Good job. I'll drink my coffee and then we will head over to the first family." he took a sip of his drink and smiled. "We'll start from the furthest address and then come back this way to the closest. So, who is first?"

Derek opened his notebook and ran his finger down the page.

"That would be Mrs Ham. The mother of the one of the twenty. Her son, Graham, was the fifth one at the hospital complaining about stomach cramps. He died only six hours after arrival."

"Alright. Let's see Mrs Ham."

They arrived at a small house on the edge of the street of Roseville. The house was crumbling from age, and ivy had climbed all over the face of the building. "Do you think she lives alone?" Derek wondered.

"Yes, probably," he replied, climbing out of his car. "Come on. Let's make sure that we find out who wanted these people dead."

"That's the problem, though, isn't it? They weren't all working for the company. Some of those used the candles as gifts."

"Not to mention the families that used the candles during the power cuts. I know what is at stake," Joe grumbled.

Derek apologised and went to knock on the door. It wasn't more than a few moments that the door quickly swung open, revealing a middle-aged woman in her mid-thirties. Her hair was light brown and her slim figure stood in the doorway.

"Are you Mrs Ham?" Derek asked, looking a little puzzled.

"Of course not." She huffed indignantly. She turned her head and bellowed down the long, narrow hall. "Mum, it's for you!"

A slightly older woman entered the hall from a small opening to the left of the corridor. She had grey hair tied into a bun and wore a loose shirt and a pair of blue jeans. "Hello? Are you the gentleman that I spoke to on the phone?" she greeted, wasting no time,

Derek nodded, reaching out to shake her hand. "Yes. I am so sorry about your loss. We are doing everything we can to find out who had done this."

"Thank you," she sighed. Her eyes were red and puffy from crying. "Please come in."

They stepped inside the house, wiping their feet on the doormat so not to tread in any unwanted mess. The floors were lined with laminate tiles and the walls were painted an off-white colour that almost looked beige.

"What do you need?" she demanded. She pulled out a folder and placed it in front of her. "I have pictures of everyone he was close to over the last few years. Some of them work with him, others not so much but had kept in touch."

"May I see?" Derek asked, giving her a small smile.

"Of course, anything I can do to help."

"I don't suppose Adelia is one of the friends she had?" Joe asked.

The woman thought for a moment, leaning over a small glass coffee table in the center of the sofas. It was made of clear glass, was round and looked almost new. The center of the table had a place mat and a tray. The woman smiled, signalling to the tray on the table. On it was a small teapot and three tea cups. "Would you like some?" she offered.

Joe smiled, "Yes, I wouldn't mind a tea. Thank you, you are very kind."

"You're welcome," she smiled. "I don't recall an Adelia. Did she work for us as well?"

Joe sighed, supping at his cup of tea. "We are not sure. Someone we spoke to suggested that she may have been a victim as well. But did not share the details of where to find her. But, this person is under the assumption that she is dead. At the minute, she may be the key to working out who is behind this. In any case, she could be the culprit, or she could be the victim. But without knowing if she is alive or dead, has put a bit of limitations on what we know."

"So, she could be the victim of these candles, and no one knows where she is? That is horrible!"

Derek drained his tea and placed his cup on the table. "It certainly is. Hopefully, we can find her. For now, though, is there anyone else or anyone that may have openly threatened your son? Did he have any problems at work?"

"Not really, but Graham rarely spoke about work. He always looked quite agitated after he comes home though."

"Where did he keep his candle, please?"

"It is in his bedroom, upstairs, first door on the right. It is opposite the bathroom."

"Thank you, Mrs Ham," Derek replied. He stood up slowly and climbed the stairs. He took a deep breath, reached the top of the corridor, and opened the bedroom door.

Inside the bedroom was a single bed pushed up against the wall. His pillow overlooked the view of outside the bedroom window. A large jar candle sat perched on the window seel, just inches away from where Graham's head would have been. "There it is," he sighed. He grabbed the candle and put it into a bag before heading back down the stairs.

Mrs Ham was still talking to Joe about the pictures in the photo album. "I know the pictures are all online, kept on tablets and phones these days. But once the memory is full, we like to print off our favourite ones so that we don't lose them."

"That sounds like a wonderful idea. I should think about doing that," Joe cheered.

"Thank you." She turned to Derek with a sad smile. "Have you got what you needed?"

Derek nodded, holding the evidence bag up. "Yes, right here. If the killer left any prints, we'll find it."

"Alright. I hope you do." the woman sighed, sniffing back her tears.

"I'll call you when I have anything to tell you." Derek smiled. He opened the front door and stepped out. Joe followed, thinking hard about what they had spoken about. "I am wondering if Adelia had any friends."

"From what I have heard, I don't think she did."

"I agree. And the more we look into this, the more I think she might be the key to this entire case. Either way, we need to find her."

They climbed into the car and thought some more. "We need to ask someone who knew her better. So perhaps her boss. Surely he would know if there was anyone who liked her- although I'm guessing that the conversation would only confirm what we suspect. And if she is as unliked as we think, she may very well be the killer. Especially if they were trying to kill her first."

"And with any luck, we can find her before they succeed in following it through." Derek agreed.

They arrived at the Loan Industries once again to find people in an uproar by the entrance. Their boss, Mr Handler, was standing by the front entrance, trying to calm the raging crowd.

"What the hell is going on here?" Derek pondered, mostly thinking out loud.

"I assume that by now, everyone has heard that people are dying, and expect the boss to do something about it," Joe guessing, shrugging his shoulders.

"It is too dangerous to work here now!" someone argued. "There are only a few of us left!"

"Yes, I know!" Carl replied, getting frustrated. "And I appreciate you are all worried about your families. But I am doing everything the police will allow."

"Has anyone heard from Adelia? She used to work here too! She should hear this!" a man announced angrily.

"No one has heard from Adelia since she has left. I am not sure if she is even alive at this point. Speaking of which, there are rumours that people within this company had tried to have her killed. I have several reports on my desk that her life was almost taken. Her house, included, as from last night, was set on fire. It was a good thing that she wasn't in there. As my employees, I am expecting you all to behave sensibly than turn into hooligans, thugs, and murderers!"

"Does anyone even like her?" Derek demanded, raising his voice over the agitated crowd.

As though he had spoken something truly horrifying, the crowd fell silent. "Seriously?" Joe frowned. "You're all eager to say something, but not one of you can think of someone who likes her?"

The crowd mumbled incoherently as a reply.

Taking a deep breath, Derek went to the front and showed his homicide badge. "Now, if none of you liked her. Which one of you was more tolerant of her than the rest?"

He scanned the faces in front of him, only to be met with uncomfortable silence. "Oh, jeez. No wonder someone wants you lot dead-you're all awful!"

Joe glared at him and joined him at the front. "What he meant was, how the hell are we supposed to find out if she is involved or not, if no one here is decent enough to speak about her?" He glared hard at

Derek, who was looking as uncomfortable as the crowd. "Right?" he demanded, giving him a hard nudge.

"Yes, that is what I was getting at," he grumbled.

"Well, I suppose that would be me," a voice sighed with heavy reluctance. "I barely spoke to her, but that also meant I was kinder to her, I suppose... if that makes any sense?"

"Not really, but I appreciate you coming forward. Do you know where she kept her files and I don't suppose you know where she lives?"

"It would be in the office. The boss would have her address, but it would be pointless. The boss said that her house was torched last night, and she wasn't in it."

"Yes, he did, didn't he..." Joe said thoughtfully. "So, all I need to do is track down all the fires that happened in the area last night. That shouldn't be too hard..."

"So I can go back to work?" the fourth comer asked.

"What is your name first?" Joe asked, getting out his notepad.

"It's Simon. Simon Dealy. Now can I go?"

Joe shrugged, "Yeah, I guess. I will catch up with you later, no doubt. Don't go on any holidays. I may need to ask you some more questions." After taking out his phone, he called the fire department office and asked to speak to the fire marshal. He was put on hold and left to wait. He grumbled, listening to the sounds of violin playing in the background as the default hold music that he grew to hate.

A few minutes passed when someone on the line finally spoke. "What can I do for you?"

"Hello Marshal. I was wondering how many buildings were on fire last night. That was in the area?"

"Why?" he demanded. "Who are you?"

"I'm Detective Joe Twit. There's someone that might be involved in the deaths of dozens of people. I heard her house was set on fire last night."

"Then you would need to be more specific. There was a few."

"Uh, this one would be empty. Someone has been trying to kill her, though so far they have been unsuccessful, as far as I know."

"There was only one empty house that was on fire. It was on the corner of fourth and second street opposite the pizza place."

"Awesome. Thank you. I don't suppose you know what was used to set the fire?"

"Just some petrol," the marshal replied.

"Were there any candles in a jar, maybe scented and unused?"

"Hard to tell. The whole place was in flames."

"Then it was a good thing you were all wearing your suits. The candle was poisonous. But that would also wouldn't rule her out as the victim either."

"Was there anything you could tell us that might help?"

"Only that a lot of her stuff was cleared out. Her clothes mostly, so I guess she was going to be staying somewhere else for a while. Now, she would have to stay somewhere else a little longer than planned."

"Yes, that certainly looks like it." Joe sighed. "Thank you."

He hung up the phone and groaned. "That was no help at all, other than that this proves that either someone was trying to kill her or that she tried to get rid of evidence. We are no closer to finding out if she is the culprit or the victim in this!"

"So, it proves one thing."

"What does it prove?"

"That she is definitely the key to this whole mess."

Adelia looked around the dark street, eyeing the time on her watch. It was almost eleven o'clock at night. She sighed, wearily searching for a familiar face. As though she was being watched, her phone rang. "How is it looking?" she whispered.

There was a muffled voice at the other end of the line. "That's great news," Adelia smiled. She looked around, frowning. "Are you nearby?"

The muffled voice replied once again. She could barely make the words out through the cheap speakers on her phone. "Alright. Start with the next step," she instructed. "We are going to cause a lot of dra-ma soon, and I want to witness it all."

Chapter 17

The Detectives headed to the Adelia's house, not quite sure what to be expecting. As they neared the corner of the road, a strong stench of what smelled like a bonfire, hung in the air. "Damn, that stinks!" Derek gasped, rolling up his window.

"Yeah, I know. We wouldn't be smelling it though if you had left the window rolled up."

"But it was getting hot in here. The windows were foggying up." Derek complained.

"It's cold outside. I'm not driving in an ice box."

"I like the cold," Derek grumbled. "And besides, it was already an ice box when we got in. That blast of cold air didn't help warm it up either."

Joe groaned, trying to stay calm. He took a deep breath, but his eye had already started to twitch. "You're right. Next time, you can drive yourself to the scenes. Or even better, walk. I hear it's going to be a frosty one again."

Derek rolled his eyes but said nothing, pressing his lips shut. He turned around trying to find something to steer the subject. It didn't take long. "There it is," he pointed. "I wonder why it is still smoking," he wondered. "Surely it couldn't have been that bad, right?"

Joe looked out of the window to where Derek was pointing and gasped. A trail of almost black smoke rose up from the ashes and charcoal. The building was burnt down to the bare bones. He could count almost to twenty bricks that remained untouched by the scortching of the flames. The flooring was covered with soot and the funiture was covered with singes and burns. Joe sighed again, as he began to wonder if Adelia had set the fire at all.

"We really need to find her," Derek stated. "This is bad."

Detective Twit nodded, digging his hands into his pockets. "Yeah. Come on, we have to look for that candle."

"Do you think she would keep one for herself?" Derek frowned, following Joe inside.

"I don't know. She may be a victim, or she may be the killer. She may be out of this all together and simply on the run because people are trying to kill her. But we won't know until we find her. And if everything is burnt..."

"Then how do we expect to find where she went?" Derek frowned, looking somewhat puzzled. He tilted his head, hoping to shift his perspective a little so he could see whatever his partner was seeing.

"I am looking for little hidey holes. It would be well protected, like in the wall or under a floorboard," Joe replied.

"Alright. I look high, and you look low."

"Sure. And then you can check upstairs whilst I look in the living room." Joe grinned. "Don;t forget the bathroom. There are probably some candles in there."

Derek reluctantly agreed and made his way up the stairs. Each step creaked and groaned. He grumbled to himself, looking at what was left of the structure skeleton. "I bet this was a really nice house, before people ruined it."

Joe shurgged, "It was OK."

"How do you know?" he pondered, looking at his partner with intrest.

"Because I use to live there," Joe replied. "About fifteen years ago."

"You lived in her house? That's fucked up," Derek replied.

"Yeah, kinda is." Joe frowned. "It's a shame that it's burnt down. The rooms were quite spacious, and it had an open plan for each room.

There weren't many doors. So the only doors it had was to the bedroom, toilet and bathroom."

"It does sound nice," Derek commented. He stepped over the rubble and went to look inside.

Inside the house, Joe looked around sadly. He could still see the carpet that had almost completely burnt up. The deep red fabric skattered around the rooms. The windows were covered with thick soot, and the walls were crumbling around them as though it were made of paper. He sighed, blinking away the memories of settling in and gardening. It was a brief stay, but it had been a few good years before getting married and moving to the house he was now in. He made his way to what used to be the living room. The gap in the wall where the window use to be, overlooked the now over-grown garden. He turned to his left to a corner, where the television would have been. He knelt down to his knees and uncovered the cable box that he had installed when he moved in. It now looked warn. He smiled, glad that it was put to good use after he left. Above the plug, was a burnt table was a bunrt out candle. He sighed, grabbed a evidence bag and placed the candle inside. "I found it," he announced.

"Oh good. We can get out of here." Derek cheered eagerly.

Joe nodded, "I will be right with you."

Derek frowned, watching as Joe headed out to the end of the garden and tugged at a handful of weeds before throwing it aside. Underneath the weeds, was a circular stepping stone. It was engraved with a name, now unrecognisable, with the letters R. I. P.

After a few moments, he got up and walked away looking grim. "It was my dog," he explained, not waititng to be asked.

"It's not...?"

"Oh. No, my dog wasn't buried here. It's just a memorial stone." Joe replied.

"Then, take it back. Take it with you," Derek prompted.

"I can't. It is not my house any more," Joe sighed. "And it would be like moving someone's grave stone. It's immoral and wrong."

Derek shrugged, "Suit yourself. Ready to go?"

Joe looked down at the evidence bag and nodded. "Yeah. Let's go."

Just as they were about to climb into the car, they notice a shadowed figure loitering in the background by the house. Suspisious, they paused and slowly began to circle and approach it. As they got closer, the shadowed figure slowly began to get clearer. Almost on top of it, they could see that it was a man.

"Who are you and what are you doing here?" Derek demanded.

"I am Thomas. I'm looking for Adelia. Is she here?"

Joe frowned, guesturing towards the burnt down rubble of what used to be a nice house. "Does it look like she is here? There's nothing left other than the skeltal structure. Perhaps you knew that though and came to get something else?"

"Like what?" he frowned, stepping back.

"Like maybe you dropped something from burning the house down, or maybe you were the one sending candles to people."

Thomas stepped back, horrifyed and tearful. "You think I did this? You think I made those fucking candles?!" he screamed. "Those candles killed my damn family, you sick fuck!"

Joe eyed him carefully, tilting his head as he thought. "What did you say your surname was?" he asked. He could feel a slight spark in his brain, something that he could almost remember.

"Wilson," he replied. "Thomas Wilson."

Joe blinked, "Right, I remember now." He turned to Derek, who still looked puzzled. "Remember at the hospital, a mother and baby died?"

Derek gasped, "Ooh, you're the husband and father that works at Loan Industries. We are trying to find her. She had a candle too, but we can't find her. There are rumours that she's dead. But without finding her body, we can't be sure. Did you know her?"

Thomas nodded, "Yeah. She's the one that everyone hates. It's because she is too good at her job. Whoever suceeded in killing her, is not my problem. I want the one that made those damn candles. I will find who killed my family and I will make them pay."

"I wouldn't recommend revenge. Let us do our job and get justice."

"Justice won't give me back my family." he scowled.

"Neither will revenge," Joe replied.

"I have nothing left, Detective. I will find her, regardless. If anyone knows who did this, it'll be her. And if she is dead, then I will just go to the next best person. The company, who allowed this to happen. I will bring the whole company to their knees within hours."

"Please, let us find out who made those candles, then you can watch them squirm in court."

"They won't make it to court. Trust me on that. But fine, i'll let you find who did this and keep out of your way. After that though, all bets are off."

Joe nodded, and pulled Derek to the car. "I think we will need to keep an eye on him."

Derek looked at him and nodded in agreement. "Yeah, this could be trouble."

Joe looked at the time on his wrist watch and sighed. "You know what, I think it's coming towards the evening. It'll be getting dark soon."

"What are you thinking?" Derek asked.

"I am thinking of heading ove to the cafe and getting some food. And then maybe see one more person before heading home for the night. We can pick up again early tomorrow. Around seven thirty? I think we need to find Adelia before any one else does."

"You're right. We can think on how to find her once we have food in our guts."

"Yeah, and it would help if we can find someone that has a picture of her. If we don't know what she looks like, we may have passed her by before already."

"I hadn't thought of that. All right. Food and then photos. Sounds simple enough, doesn't it?"

Joe nodded, "It does. Which is why I think this won't be easy at all. I think it is going to be a hard task. No one wants a picture of someone they don't like."

"You know who would have a picture, no matter what?" Joe asked, suddenly having an idea.

"Who?"

"Parents. Adelia's parents would know where she is, who she speaks to and also, have a photograph. Because, what kind of parent has no pictures of their kids?"

"You have a really good point." Derek cheered. "I can not believe that we didn't think of this sooner."

"So, we'll have dinner, and then we will try and find out the location of Adelia's mum and dad."

"That sounds like a better plan, and a lot less complicated."

Outside, the trees were bare. The leaves were brown, dry and crumbling on the grass around it, scattered from the wind. Joe shivered, entering a small diner across the street near the police station.

Inside the diner was a row of small circular tables, surrounded by larger retangular and square tables. Joe picked a circular table near the front and sat down.

"This is where we are sitting?" Derek asked, slightly irked.

"Yes, it is closer to the food," he replied, smiling. "I can smell the roast from here. Though, I think I will be having a bacon sandwich with a pot of coffee."

They left the diner half an hour later. Derek was still finishing his last mouthful of his fried eggs and chips, licking his lips afterwards.

"Now to find the parents..." Joe mused.

"How are we going to find that out, escatkly?" Derek wondered.

Joe thought, scratching his stubbly chin. "We'll find out her surname and go to the registry office. The birth certificates will have the parents names on them. Then we can check on social media or the council office for an address."

"Without a warrant?" Derek asked, cynically. He knew the answer to that one.

"I guess we had better get a warrant then, hadn't we." Joe sighed. "It'll take a few hours. We can call for the warrant and find out where to go tomorrow morning. We need to do this early."

Derek agreed and got on to the phone to ask the judge, crossing his fingers in hope that they would agree.

After a brief explaination, the court agreed on the warrant to find the address. It was now pitch black dark outside. Joe could less only five lights were working, and more than half were either broken or was in need of a new lightbulb. With all the power cuts, he wasn't surprised the lights were getting faulty. He frowned, the power cut hasn't happened in a while. He shrugged, thinking to himself. "I wonder how they fixed the power cuts."

Derek blinked, "What?"

Joe laughed, "I was talking to myself. I was just thinking about the power cuts. There hadn't been any for a while. I wonder what was causing them."

"I don't know. But I am grateul for the working electronics. I have read all my books now, and if the electric went, I would have nothing else to read.

"Oppose to having something to read with the lights on?"

"Yeah, it is called an ebook. Plenty of free ones out there." Derek cheered.

Joe shook his head and turned away. "Time to go home. We have another busy day tomorrow. This case is starting to look like a dead end. So I hope we have something soon."

They said goodnight and went their separate ways.

Derek got home and walked into the living room. "Where is my wife?" he muttered. The lights were off and the television was off as well. His home seemed to be empty. He glanced down at the time on his watch. It was almost midnight. It was not like her to stay out for so long. Just as he was getting out of his work clothes, and climbed into his bed. He wasn't about to stay up for the sake of it. He sighed, "I'll be having words with her tomorrow," he told himself with a yawn.

It was almost three hours before he heard the door unlock and footsteps climbing slowly up the stairs. He barely opened his eyes, seeing the shadowy figure of his wife climbing gently into bed next to him. Her skin pressed against his. He wrinkled his nose, a strong smell inches from his nose, irritating his senses. He frowned, it wasn't perfume. He knew all of the perfume that he had given her in the past, and there wasn't many. He cleared his throat, his eyes still closed in his half-asleep state. That smell clung to her, had a more masculine scent to it. He swallowed hard. Was he really suspecting his wife of cheating? A knot gnawed at his stomach. Who had she been with? Why does she smell like another man? He shook his head, foreigning a nightmare he couldn't wake from. The last thoughts in his head, before falling asleep raced through his mind. Who was sleeping with his wife?

Chapter 18

J oe got home and headed straight into the kitchen. Megan was
standing by the kettle, waiting for him. "How did your day go?" she
asked, hoping for a sympathetic response.

"Well, we think we have thought of a way to find someone that had
been eluding us. So we could wrap this case up pretty soon."

"That is great news," Megan smiled.

He nodded, watching as she walked closer to him. He could hear
the sounds of her feet shuffling forward as her slippers dragged along
the tile flooring. She leaned forward, planting a gentle kiss on his lips.

"As long as we can find her, that is great. Otherwise, we'd be no closer to ending this thing. It's already taken two weeks to get this far."

They stayed up watching the television until ten and switched it off.
Joe yawned, dreading what was likely waiting for him. He could only
close his eyes and hope that things would get better.

The sun beamed brightly through the bedroom window. Joe woke,
shivering under his blanket. "Damn, it's so cold!"

Megan rolled over, wrapping herself up tightly in the blanket,
groaning in her sleep.

Defeated by the cold, he decided it was time to wake up and get
dressed. He climbed out of bed and grabbed his clothes from the
wardrobe, including a thick black jumper from his top drawer. He
stepped back, making sure the rest of the three drawers of the cabinet
were closed properly before changing.

Once dressed, he made his way down the stairs towards the kitchen
and grabbed the largest coffee mug from the cupboard. He switched

the coffee machine on, and sat down on a stall as he waited, pulling it out from under the kitchen unit.

The smell of coffee greeted him like an old friend as the aroma filled the room. He poured the drink into his favourite zombie mug before he added a splash of milk and stirred it in, absentmindedly thinking about the case. He sighed. Even with the warrant, he may not get the address, but he hoped so.

He left quietly, closing the door behind him, careful not to wake his wife from her sleep. He walked down the stony path, wrinkling his nose in disgust. They cluttered the pathway with rubbish bags that had been split in the middle of the night. Claw marks tore into the plastic as though they had made it with paper, scattering the litter and left over food across the pavement. He gagged and covered his nose, trying to avoid the overpowering stench of the liquid that had leaked out from the black bags.

As soon as he climbed into his car, he closed the door and breathed a sigh of relief, being met with the sweet smell of vanilla that hung in his mirror.

Detective Joe Twit pulled away from the curb and made his easy to the station, hoping that Derek would wait for him when he arrives.

His mind wondered to the parents of Adelia, wondering what they would look like, and what their thoughts would be on the matter. Would they talk of how innocent she is, or would they fear the visits from them and listen with dread? His mouth twisted to the side as he thought, almost missing the corner traffic light turn amber and then red. He stopped and secured the car, putting his attention back into driving.

He finally arrived at the station to find that he was the first one to turn up. The street was still dark, and the sky was still a murky grey. He sighed, switched his car off, and sat in silence as he waited.

A few minutes passed before Derek arrived, driving his ford focus into the parking lot.

"Are you ready to, finally, end this?" Derek asked, calling out to him.

"Yes. I can't wait until we can put this nightmare behind us," Joe agreed, all too eagerly.

They stepped out of their cars and headed into the station, filled with determination.

They walked into the office to collect the warrant and then got ready to head over to the council office. Joe remained silent, still mulling around the thoughts in his head about what to expect. "I hope this won't be a waste of time," he grumbled. He dusted off a loose strand of hair from his coat and narrowed his eyes. Of course, it belonged to his wife, who was constantly losing her hair- and he was finding it everywhere more and more frequently. He wondered how she still had hair left on her head, but it would have been rude to ask such things. He smirked to himself, envisioning the slap that he would have gotten if he had.

They arrived at the building and walked over to the front desk. A woman was sitting facing a computer. Her shoulders were hunched over and her expression looked bleak and bored.

"Can I help you with something?" the woman asked, looking up at them. She had short, grey curly hair and half-moon glasses perched on the end of her nose.

"Yes please, we need to know the address of Adelia Lake's parents?"

"I can't help you with that," she replied, looking back down at her computer keyboard.

"Yes, of course you can. I have a warrant here that says that you can help me."

"Alright fine, where is the warrant?"

Derek handed her the sheet of paper and waited.

She sighed, glancing at it, and then typed on her computer again. "What is her full name?"

"I dunno, Mrs Lake?" Derek answered off handedly.

"You don't know her name?"

Joe sighed, stepping forwards to see if he could do any better.

"What about Adelia Lake? She used to work for Loan Industries- that'll be on the system, wouldn't it- because of taxes?"

She looked at him with a hard glare. "Is your warrant for Adelia or her parents?"

"Her parents," Derek replied. "Because we need to know her address and find out where her daughter is."

"Then I can not tell you anything about Adelia and only tell you what I mentioned on the warrant." She stated firmly. She tapped her foot as she waited for her computer to load.

"Mrs Lake with a daughter called Adelia... the birth certificate says she lived in Southend Peek. Her current address, though, is downtown Manhattan, Mulan City." She printed the address off and handed it to the detectives. She then immediately went back to her computer to finish doing her work.

Joe raised an eyebrow, glimpsing the screen. A distinguishable blue letter was at the top of the screen. "Have fun on social media," he sniped. "I am sure your boss wouldn't want to slacking off during office hours."

She shot him a hard look, narrowing her eyes to small slits and then turned her computer screen so that he couldn't see what she was doing.

Joe laughed and turned away, heading out of the building with the address in his hand. "Now, let's find Adelia and get this over with."

They walked back out into the cold, with the grey murky sky still looming above them, threatening to rain.

Joe looked down at the name of the city that Mrs Lake was living in and tilted his head. "You know what it looks like to me?"

Derek shrugged. "Nope."

"It looks like someone got drunk and tried to spell Manhattan. But then thought, heck, I got it wrong- we'll leave it as it is and call somewhere else Manhattan instead."

"Yeah, I can actually imagine that," Derek laughed. "On a Friday night, drinking the night away whilst trying to reach a deadline."

They laughed and then slowed into an awkward silence.

"I think me and my wife are having some troubles..." Derek commented sadly.

"About the cheating thing?" Joe prompted.

Derek nodded, "Yeah. I am trying to move past it, and try to save the relationship. But, it is all I can think about. I don't look at her the same way anymore. When I look at her, all I can see is her being intimate with another man. It's breaking my heart."

"You need to talk to her," Joe replied. "If it feels like the relationship is over, then it is probably time to end it. You would only do yourselves more harm than good to stick with it."

Derek looked down at the ground, blinking, as if he was trying to see something more. "Yeah, I suppose you're right. I will speak to her tonight."

"Until then, let's talk to the mother whilst it is still early."

They climbed into the car and pulled away once more, heading to the town of drunken mistakes. They crossed the state and headed over the bridge and then through the countryside until they reached the edge of the border and the train station.

Joe looked at Derek with a questioning look. "It looks like we are going to catch the train."

Joe looked at the timetable pinned to a lamppost and watched as the time changed for each train to that station. "It says we have around five minutes before it is due."

The platform got crowded, cramming around the track, ready to grab the train as soon as it arrives.

"I hope the journey wouldn't be too long," Joe grumbled. He looked at the time on his watch. To get across two states has taken them six and a half hours. "Damn, we missed lunch," he huffed, clutching his noisy, growling stomach. "It's almost three o'clock!"

"It took that long?" Derek gasped.

Joe nodded. "So much for doing this thing quickly. It's going to be almost the end of our shift by the time we get back."

The bell rang, signalling to the passengers that the train was almost there and about to pull in.

"Do you think there would be food on the train?"

Joe scoffed, "Of course not. This isn't a train to wizard school- more like the cheaper version of the Orient express?"

"Ah, if only it was. That would make our lives so much easier. A flick of the wrist and everything would be as it is supposed to be. Effortless."

Chapter 19

The train pulled into the station and the doors slid open. The carriage was crammed with people, squeezed in like sardines.

Joe stepped inside the train and hung on to the roped handle hanging over his head. He cringed and held on to it, feeling the stickiness on the plastic from other people's sweat. As he held his breath, trying to breathe as little as possible, bodies pushed against him. He swallowed hard, closing his eyes tight. A large man next to him raised his arm, holding on to the handle beside him. He wrinkled his nose. He heaved, feeling nauseous as a wave of body odour from a sweaty arm pit hovered inches from his nose.

The train slowed to a stop three hours later and pulled onto the next platform. Joe scrambled for the door, gasping for breath. When the door slid open, he rushed outside, feeling the fresh air on his face. He took a long, deep breath, sucking in the crisp, cold air. "That was disgusting," he complained, turning to Derek.

Derek laughed, stretching his legs as he walked. "It wasn't that bad. I actually found somewhere to sit."

"You're kidding? I was standing for the entire journey, next to someone who smelled like he hadn't washed in a year!"

"Well, where do we go from here?" Derek prompted, eager to change the subject.

"According to this map, we need to go halfway across town. So, I am guessing the next stop will get a bus or get a taxi?"

"The buses are cheaper, but could be as bad as the train journey. So, I vote for the taxi."

"I agree. Let's call the taxi then and hopefully get to the house before it gets dark?"

"It won't be long. It's almost half five now," Derek replied.

"Precisely my point, and we hadn't even eaten or had any coffee since this morning."

"Yeah, I noticed. My stomach hasn't shut up since we got to the train station. I am forking out for a massive pizza when I get home later."

"As soon as we dealt with the mother, we can go home," Joe stated.

Derek frowned. "Why not eat now whilst we wait for the taxi?"

"Do you think we have time for that?" Joe pondered.

"We don't know how long the taxi will take to turn up?

Why not go somewhere where there is food and call from there? If they say it is a long wait, we can eat and be back before the taxi even gets here."

Joe sighed. He had a good point. "Alright fine. But if we miss the taxi, you can pay for the fare back."

They looked around the area, making a mental note of their surroundings. They walked up a flight of stairs and came to a cross junction. In the top right corner, there was a small coffee shop. Opposite that was the beauty parlour. Joe turned around, frowning. Beauty would not fill their stomachs. On the bottom left was a pizza shop, which he thought was do-able. Opposite that was the Chinese takeaway shop. He thought for a moment, considering his options. "I actually wouldn't mind a curry right now," he stated.

Derek fell silent, which was a rare occurrence, biting his top lip as he weighed the options. "Yeah, I suppose a korma wouldn't kill me."

"A korma? I was thinking chicken tikka," Joe laughed.

Derek shrugged his shoulders. "Good thing we're not sharing. We clearly have different tastes."

Joe agreed and headed over to the curry house, watching for unwanted traffic. The lights turned red, and he crossed the road, thankful for the traffic light filtered junction.

They bought their dinners and sat on a bench to eat.

After they finished, they called for a taxi and waited. It was almost twenty minutes before the taxi arrived and another thirty-five minutes to get to Adelia's parents' address.

Joe and Derek climbed out of the taxi and payed the driver, watching the vehicle speed away.

They stood outside a block of flats, counting the floors.

"I don't suppose she's on the first floor?" Derek hoped.

Joe looked at the address and sighed heavily. "132, so I am guessing she's closer to the top floor."

"Yeah, I thought that might be the case," he grumbled. "Why can't we have someone on the ground floor for once? People we need to talk to is always near the damn top floor."

"Just lucky, I guess." Joe scratched his head, arching his head to look up as high as he could. "But with this thirty something floor building, I am leaning towards not so lucky."

"No shit."

They went inside the building and were immediately greeted with the stench of stale urine. On their right was the flight of stairs. On their left was the elevator. Joe shook his head, trying not to read the profane words spray painted to the front of the doors. He pushed the up button with the edge of his sleeve, not wanting to touch it with his bare hands. He cringed and stepped back, already regretting his decision not to take the stairs. The elevator door opened, and they stepped inside.

Joe took a deep breath, instantly regretting his choices. "I... Uh... think I might take the stairs," he stammered.

"What's the matter?" Derek frowned, sounding puzzled.

"Are you not seeing this? It looks like something out of a horror movie. Graffitied doors and flickering lights- it looks like a death trap!"

"You're not a claustrophobic, are you?" Derek prompted.

Joe scoffed, looking away towards the exit. "Of course not. Look at this place. It's unclean and filthy. The lift is probably temperamental. There is no way I am gonna be in that box if the cable wire snaps."

"You're being ridiculous," Derek laughed. "Come on. We'll be up there in no time. But if you are that concerned, we can take the stairs on the way down."

Joe thought for a moment. The stairs going down sounded a lot better than climbing the stairs to the top. He took a deep breath and swallowed a hard, dry lump in his throat. "Fine, but if we die, I am dragging you to hell."

"Alright," Derek chuckled. "If we die, I'll even let you stab me with a pitchfork."

They stepped inside the box and pushed the highest number at the top of the panel. "Floor 28," Joe instructed in a shaky voice.

Joe watched as the doors slid closed. The floor below him lurched up and down as it moved between floors. He gripped the handle railing tightly, breathing with shaky rasped breaths.

Derek watched him with concern. "Are you alright?" he asked. "You look a little pale and clammy."

"I'm fine," he squeaked. "Just a minor panic attack."

Derek sighed, putting a hand on his colleague's shoulder. "It is going to be all right. We'll be at the top quickly, and then we can take the stairs to the bottom."

Joe nodded. "Are we there yet?"

"Count to twenty," Derek smiled.

Joe nodded again, taking a deep breath as he counted. "One...Two...Three..."

He closed his eyes, focusing on the numbers. "Eighteen... Nineteen...Twenty." The elevator pinged, and the doors opened. Not wasting any time, he rushed out of the metal box on to the corridor and went to stand in the open space by the row of front doors.

"That wasn't too bad, was it?" Derek smiled.

Joe shot him a glare, grumbling incoherently under his breath. "I am sure there are things you're not a fan of, too."

"Sure, all the time. I'm not a fan of bugs. But I don't spend enough time outside to see anything."

Joe shook his head. "We are always outside."

"Yes, but we're surrounded by concrete. No risk of spider nests or hornets."

"Hornet?"

"Yeah, horrid things. Flying bugs, really. Hate them."

They headed towards the front door, double checking that they had the right number before knocking. Itching to get this over with, they knew it was now dark outside, and the street below was lit up with street lights.

"Lets get this over with," Joe huffed. "I don't want to stick around."

Derek knocked on the door and waited.

Joe stepped beside his partner, hearing heavy footsteps approach the front door, thudding along the floorboards.

The door opened, revealing a frumpy-looking woman. She had curly greying hair, an apple shaped frame and flat canvas shoes.

Joe raised an eyebrow, trying not to stare at her baggy jeans and loose fitting t-shirt that age had stained and spilt coffee.

"Who the fuck are you?" she demanded irritably. "I was about to have a bath."

"Uh, sorry. Are you Adelia's mother?"

"Not sure if you can call me that, but yes. I gave birth to her, so I suppose I am."

"Hm. I am guessing you're not friendly at the minute, then?"

"Look, I love her. She is my kid. But she has my attitude, which stinks. Not one of my loveliest traits, but that's not how it works, is it? You don't pick what traits they get born with."

"Oh, I see. I don't suppose you know where she is?" Joe questioned. "We need to find her. She might be in trouble. We believe her life is being threatened."

"That would explain a lot. She came to me the other day. Someone had set fire to her house. Thankfully, she wasn't inside. She had just got to the corner of her road when it happened. So, it was a close call. If she had been home a couple of minutes sooner, she would have died—"

"You said you saw her?" Joe interrupted.

"Yes. I gave her money for an RV. Lovely vehicle, it was. So she can move about without losing her home."

"An RV? That's nice. Do you know the licence plate?"

She beamed, "Of course. I took a picture." She pulled her phone out and flicked through her photographs.

As quickly as she smiled, her smile disappeared and turned into a look of disappointment. The images were there, but none of them had the licence plate visible. "Oh, I'm sorry," she sighed. "I thought it would be in the pictures. Unfortunately, I must have aimed a little higher than I thought. I really am sorry."

Joe shrugged. "That's fine. There can't be many RVs around. Hey, I don't suppose you have a picture of your daughter?"

She flicked through the camera photos again until she came across a picture of a young woman standing beside the RV. "Here. This got taken three days ago."

She sent the picture to Joe's phone with bluetooth and put the phone back into her pocket. "I am sorry I couldn't be any more help."

Derek smiled. "That's OK. We've got something to go on now. I am sure we can find her and make sure that she is alright."

They left the flat and made their way to the stairwell. Joe sighed, waved her goodbye and descended the stairs. He wrinkled his nose, noting the stairs smelled like a toilet.

Joe raced down the stairs, quickly feeling nauseous from the smell. His heart pounded as he raced down, jumping two steps at a time.

"Wait for me!" Derek called out, panting hard behind him.

Derek gasped, jumping the stairs, trying to catch up to him as he raced ahead.

The walls were covered with spray paint, and the floor was sticking to the souls of their shoes. Joe cringed, trying not to think about what he could tread in, and instead focused on understanding the stairs and out of the building, into the open fresh air.

When they finally reached the bottom, Joe launched himself out into the open, gasping for air. He took a few breaths and then turned to his partner. "Well, now we have an idea what and who to look for."

Derek nodded, glancing at his smart watch on his wrist. "Yeah, that is true. And it is now almost seven o'clock. That took a lot longer than I thought it would. By the time we get home, it is going to be almost ten."

"That's if we are lucky," Joe chuckled. "Come on. Let's get going, you still need to have that chat with your wife."

"That will have to wait until morning now. I am not breaking up with her in the middle of the night."

Joe smiled. "I know. But you still need to talk to her. Even if it is in the morning. And I also have a meal waiting. I hope it won't be too dry..."

They got into a taxi and made their way back to the train station, down the steps and onto the platform. Joe cringed, praying that there would be a seat available this time round, not wanting to relive the horror from the previous journey.

Chapter 20

He got on to the train, immediately scanning the coach for some empty seats. It took a few minutes and then finally saw a seat at the far end of the coach. Eagerly, he went to sit down. He stared out of the window, watching as the streetlights lit the path with a warm orange glow. Joe sighed, wishing the hours would speed by so that he could get home sooner.

It was gone ten fifteen when Joe finally got home and through his front door. He closed it, shuddering, as the journey haunted him. Though there was at least somewhere to sit on the journey back, the seat was not empty. It was better than having his nose in someone's sweaty armpit, but he still couldn't escape the foul smell of unclean strangers. He sighed, vividly remembering an old woman in the chair beside him, with a strong smell of sweaty perfume and a distinct stench of wet dog. It made him wonder where the old woman had come from, whether she had washed a dog at home, or perhaps she volunteered in an animal shelter. He shook his head. Whether it was through good intentions, the woman did not smell pleasant by any means.

He walked through the hallway, noting that the lights were all switched off. He crept along, feeling his way through beside the wall. When he made it to the other end, he switched on the kitchen light to make himself a cup of decaf coffee. He wouldn't normally consider it as an option, but it was late, and he knew he would sleep soon. The next morning was going to be just as long, and he needed whatever rest he could. Just as he poured the hot water into his zombie mug, he turned around. He recognised the soft steps of his wife's slippers and turned to face her with a tired smile.

"I hope I didn't wake you," he stated in a quiet tone.

"No, I was waiting for you to come home. Was it a bad day?"

Joe sighed. Bad wasn't the word he would have chosen. "Ah, no. It was awful. We found the suspect's mother, but she was living three states over and it took hours to get there. And the journey alone was a disaster. We had a brief visit with the mother and then made it all the way back. We literally got into town about half an hour ago. I wasted the whole day travelling."

"That sounds like a pretty rough day. So it took all day to have one conversation? Was it worth the travel?"

Joe frowned. He hadn't given it much thought. "I dunno. We now know what the suspect looks like, and we know what she is travelling in. So, I suppose it was worth it. I just wish we hadn't needed to take all day to get there."

"Was the place nice?"

"Nope. The mother's house was a dump. It was a flat on the twenty-eighth floor, and I had to go into an elevator to get to it. The lights were flickering, there was spray paint on the walls and the elevator and hall-way smelled like a public toilet."

"Ew," she replied.

"Yeah, that's what I thought. A lot."

He finished his decaf coffee and followed his wife into the bed-room, peeling off his clothes as he dropped them to the floor as he walked. He closed the door behind him and climbed into bed and un-der the covers.

Derek walked through the door to his house and took off his coat and shoes. He yawned, wincing as he stretched to hang his coat up on to its hanger. The rooms were dark, though there were muffled voices coming from the lounge at the end of the hall. The flickering lights sug-gested they had left the television on. As he neared, the voices became clearer. He held his breath so that he couldn't hear himself breathing.

Slowly, he emerged from the living room door and stood in the opening of his living room.

He stood stunned, unblinking as he watched his wife wrap her legs around a man's neck, whilst a head was planted firmly between hers.

"What the hell is this?" He demanded, his voice sounding like a loud boom. His wife jumped off the sofa, startled as though a cannon had just gone off. He stared at her, mouth open and red faced. She stood in front of him, blushing, holding a shirt against her naked body. Behind her, hiding behind the sofa, was a shadow of a man. "I can see you. Get your ass up and get out of my house."

"Please, could I just get dressed first?" the man asked sheepishly.

Derek glared at him. "My brother. This is what you had in mind when you said you were down for a visit? To sleep with my wife?!" He punched the door beside him, forcing the wood to splinter, leaving a large hole. He turned to his wife, his voice trembled. "I was going to give you a chance. I'm not stupid. But I know now, I won't waste a second chance on you. I was going to speak to you in the morning about breaking up officially and allowing you to leave—because I was nice enough to consider that it was in the middle of the night. But now, fuck you both. I am not leaving it until morning. You can both get out right now, and you, my dear wife, can leave, too. I am going to call the lawyer in the morning and you can expect the divorce papers shortly after."

"But it is in the middle of the night," she insisted. "Where am I gonna go?"

"Don't play the victim. You can go to my brother's house. You're all ready riding his dick!"

"I.. uh.. I was going to stay here with you," he stammered, now looking guilty as sin.

"You have all ready been inside my wife. There is no chance in hell that you're going to be staying in my house. I want you both out. You have five seconds to grab your clothes and leave. I don't care that you're naked. If you had worried about being seen in the nude, you would have kept your clothes on!"

Derek made his way to the kitchen and opened the fridge, then pulled out a large bottle of whisky and a small glass. "I hate people," he grumbled, and poured the alcohol to the top of the rim.

He took one last look at his now-dressed wife and brother and opened the front door. "Goodbye," he said bitterly.

He watched as they walked through the door before slamming the door firmly behind him. He gulped back his drink, and went to bed on the sofa, reminding himself to burn the sofa and the bedsheets after work the next day.

The morning came with a thick grey fog. Derek woke from his bed and poured himself a large black coffee. He climbed into the shower, changed his clothes, and got ready for work. He glanced at the time on his watch, yawning. With only got four hours of sleep, he looked like he had slept on the floor. He shook his head and looked in the mirror, combing his hair. At least now he was more presentable. He grabbed his keys and walked out of the front door, dead locking the door behind him so that his wife couldn't let herself in later.

He climbed into the car and headed to the station. He put on the radio and blared the volume, grinding his teeth into the rock music playlist.

When he arrived at the station, Joe was already waiting outside, drinking his cup of coffee. He groaned, hoping that Joe wouldn't ask how the morning or the night went. He really didn't want to talk about it.

He pulled over and climbed out of his car, and tried to fake a smile. "Good morning," he cheered. "What a great day."

"It's foggy," Joe replied, frowning. "What's great about it?"

"Uh, it adds mystery?" Derek replied, trying to stay positive.

"We're detectives, Derek. We have enough mystery in our lives." He frowned, looking at him through narrowed eyes. "You're not a perky person. What's going on?"

Derek looked at the ground and breathed out a defeated sigh. "I got home last night to find my wife screwing my brother."

"Seriously? That's messed up? What'd you do?"

"What did you think I'd do? I kicked them both out of my house, of course. I gave them five seconds to grab their shit and get out."

"Was he staying at his own house, or was he not local and booked a hotel?"

"That's the punchline," Derek laughed as he relayed the conversation from the previous night.

"Well, no wonder you kicked them out. Assholes. Are you all right?" Joe asked, offering a sympathetic smile.

"I will be. I just want to focus on this case so I can burn my bedsheets and sofa later. So, I can pick up new sofa and sheets tomorrow."

Joe nodded. Even he could understand that. He would probably make the same choices if he were in the same situation. He shifted his feet and took out his phone, admiring the picture of his wife on the screensaver. "I don't know how I would behave if my wife betrayed me like that."

"Yeah, I wouldn't recommend finding out. It hurts like a bitch," he advised.

Chapter 21

They walked into the station and checked the CCTV cameras for an RV. Joe sighed. There couldn't be much in the area. They are expensive and pretty damn big. It would be like missing a bus.

He gazed out of the window. A tiny spark of an idea formed in the back of his mind. "Maybe she would know this and try to blend in with coaches and buses instead of the major traffic route."

Derek raised his eyebrows in surprise. "That is genius!" he cheered, typing on the keyboard to look for coach trips and routes that are more common. "Here's one," he announced. "There's a route to Camberland Zoo. She might have gone that way, just before they get to Camberland. It would be all countryside for miles."

"Brilliant. Look at the CCTVs in those areas and let me know if you see any RVs heading that way. I'll grab us a coffee each."

Joe went down the hall to the staff room and switched on the coffee machine. He prepared the ground coffee and tried to remember how to use it. It was much easier to buy the coffee and not worry about using the machines. He sighed. They were so close to finding Adelia; it was hard to see what else could go wrong. He paused, deep in thought. Nothing was ever easy. Something was bound to go wrong. He just didn't know what.

He finished making the coffees and took it back to the office where Derek was waiting.

"Any luck?" Joe asked, his voice slightly elevated as he tried to sound hopeful.

"I think so," he replied. "There's an RV that looks fairly new. It just passed the Zoo a few hours ago. By now, she is in the countryside, somewhere. I just need to find out where. The problem is, there are virtually no cameras in the countryside. So, both good news and bad news."

"So, she is in an RV which is as big as a bus, but we can't find it?" Joe frowned. "This could be a problem. Come on, maybe we can find some clues where she might end up. Surely she has some sort of plan."

"I am not sure how, though."

"I do," Joe blinked. "See if you can capture the last frame the RV is in. Maybe we can get the Licence plate from the CCTV cameras."

"That is a good idea. I can't believe I didn't think of that."

"I can't believe I didn't think of it sooner, to be honest," Joe muttered.

"I have another idea," Derek blinked, getting his motivation back. "Grab me a map."

Joe handed him a paper map so that they can both see what he is showing.

He pointed to a long road in the countryside. "Look, there is only one road along the countryside, right?"

"Right."

"Well, after the long road, it doesn't split into conjoining roads again until the next village. I can search the cameras there and wait for her to go through it for a location. Maybe even beat her to it!"

Joe looked at him, stunned into silence. "So, we can get to the village before she gets there. We just need to know where the road leads?"

"That's what I am saying."

"Derek, sometimes you are smarter than you look," Joe stated proudly.

"Thank you, I think. Though I really don't know if that was a compliment or an insult. Are you saying I look stupid?"

"Don't spoil it," Joe told him with a sidewards glance. "I am only just liking you."

They looked along the map and traced their finger all the way up the road until the next location. "Hansel Village, strange name. Alright, let's go. Hopefully, we can get there before she does."

"How?" Derek asked. "She has a huge head start."

"We get some help," he smiled.

Derek looked at his partner's face, noting the mischeivious look he had. "Are you going to do something stupid?"

"Yeah, a little. Call the cops from the other side of the road and have them put a roadblock up. That way, she will have nowhere else to go."

"That is going to be a lot of paperwork."

"Yes, but it will be totally worth it."

Derek called the police station from the other side of the countryside and explained what was going on. "If our estimation is right, she should come towards your end in a couple of hours," he finished.

Joe grinned. "We almost have her. There won't be any more deadly candles and body counts after this."

"Unless she some of them has forgotten to ditch the candles," Derek replied, being more realistic. "Lets face it, not many people will listen to police officers. And we don't know how many candles are still out there."

"Put a dampener on my good mood, don't you? You couldn't just let me be happy for a little while."

"Sorry, but unless we can confirm there aren't more candles out there, the bodies might keep coming. This could be an ongoing thing for months yet."

"Ugh. Look, let's just deal with one thing at a time. And right now, we can focus on getting this one win."

"Alright, fine. Let's get her and then find out what the actual damage is, providing that we can actually get her and that she would tell us anything. It isn't likely that she is going to confess to the deaths. It's a death sentence as it is."

"It is, but maybe she doesn't know that. Maybe she thinks it will just be life in prison. Perhaps she thinks she won't get convicted at all."

"All of those deaths, including a six-month-old baby; there is no way that she will get away with it. The families will be outraged and likely take the law into the own hands."

"And end up killing her themselves? Yeah, I am pretty certain that is what would follow. Maybe she'll disappear and live a happy life. Who the fuck knows?"

"What we need to do is get her and get a damn confession. Also, we need to make sure that there is plenty of evidence to prove that she knew what she was doing, with the intent on killing them all."

"We have our work cut out for us. It will not be easy."

"Easy? Nothing about this case has been easy, Derek. It has all been a long hard slog, and I am sick of it. I am dreading the next storm we have, or the next power outage that could kill dozens more people."

"It really is a nightmare," Derek agreed. "The officers are putting up the road block now. So we should find out soon."

"Well then. Let's make our way down there with our sirens blaring. I don't want to miss all the action."

"Yup. And then before we interrogate her, we can take her back to the home town and eat. I want her sweating in a cell for a bit until we have finished our lunch."

The long road to the countryside was bendy and narrow. Edges of the road were blurred and covered with overgrown grass. The lines to mark the edge were also fading, only specks of the paint remained.

The road itself wasn't great either, as they bumped along, driving into one pothole after another, jumping over cracks and bumps of what was once been a smooth, comfortable journey.

Joe grumbled, bouncing in his seat, yelping in pain as his head bounced off the ceiling and landing back in his seat with a hard thump. "Dang it! This road is going to damage my car or I am gonna get a concussion."

"It is in the middle of nowhere. How did you think it was going to be?"

"Being in the middle of nowhere is why I would think that this road would be in better condition."

"Maybe before, but it is also one of the least travelled roads, and requires less attention. I am sure it would get fixed eventually, though."

"After someone gets a concussion?"

"Or after someone gets stuck in a pothole," Derek laughed.

"If we get stuck in a pothole, I will not be laughing," he growled.

After a while, the road opened up and they could finally see what is ahead of them. They noticed some billboards and a few shrubberies along the roadside. The road smoothed out, a hopeful sign they would arrive at the next village soon.

It was almost half an hour later, when they drove past a signpost, welcoming them to the village.

"Finally," Joe cheered. "I am dying for a coffee, and we can get off this damn road."

"Something is wrong," Derek frowned.

"What now?"

"Haven't you noticed something missing?"

"such as?"

"Such as flashing lights and a huge RV that isn't here. We should be able to see them by now."

Joe groaned. Once again, his partner had made a good point. "You're right. Where the hell is everyone?"

The dusty roads were completely deserted. The street was unlit. Even the streetlights had ceased to stop working, leaving them in complete and total darkness.

Houses could be seen silhouetted against the dark blue sky. The moon shone, allowing a small outline between the looming clouds. The stars, too, offered little light.

On the side of the road was a sign, signalling that the nearest town was less than a mile away in the east. An arrow pointed straight up to where they were heading. Another arrow pointed across the field, though there were no roads marked in the grass, pointing to Margate.

Chapter 22

They arrived at the village and were met with an empty road and an empty opening. Joe slowed down to almost a crawl, pondering on what happened to their well-designed plan to foil the woman who had killed so many people.

The streets were almost empty, other than a few people walking back home with their bags of shopping in each hand.

"Excuse me, I don't suppose you've seen an RV go by here, maybe with some police escorting them back to the station?"

The woman shook her head. "If there was anyone to be had, they wouldn't go through here. There's nothing here." Joe looked at her, observing the small and frail structure of the old woman. He thanked her for stopping and continued on their way, hoping to see something that would answer their new question. Something else that made little sense. He sighed. Something had gone horribly wrong, and his instinct screamed at him to run. He took a deep breath, bracing himself for the worst, and went to park the car.

They walked into the police station, expecting Adelia to be waiting in the cells. Joe thought hard, readying himself for the argument about who has priority over the case, since they were passing through. He straightened his back. He already knew how that would go down.

"Hello?" Joe called out, hoping for a greeting.

"Who are you?" a voice demanded angrily.

"Uh, I am Detective Joe Twit. Where's the suspect and her RV?"

"Where indeed?" a voice growled. A figure stepped out from behind a corner of the office. "We waited for five hours, blocking traffic through the road you asked us to block off. Told them to go the long way round. And we waited and waited. But the suspect and the RV never showed. A lot of paperwork for time wasting."

"She never showed? Are you sure?" Joe frowned.

"Obviously I am sure. The biggest thing that came my way was a four by four land ranger."

"I am sorry, Sherrif. Where could she have gone? There's only one road, and this is the closest village for miles."

"Unless she went across the field. That would lead her to a different village, three towns over. Basically, you've lost your suspect. She'll be long gone by now."

"That's not the news I was hoping for," Joe huffed.

"Trust me, it wasn't the turn out I was hoping for either." Derek sighed, watching as the sherif turned and headed back into his office.

"What's the town called, the one across the field?"

"Margate Peek," the sheriff called out.

Joe took the map out and looked for Margate. Sure enough, it was across the field. It wasn't a short distance either; it was quite a stretch. He huffed, "I can see why she picked this route. It gives her a massive advantage."

"Yeah, like she needed more advantages right now," Derek commented sarcastically.

"Tell me about it. We need to catch up with her, and get ahead if we can."

"I am not sure we can at this point..." Derek replied. "Not without some help. But we still don't know which way she is heading."

"Agreed," Joe replied. He closed his eyes. Thinking of what to do. "Alright. I am going to make her name and face public knowledge. If everyone knows what she looks like, and everyone knows what she has done. It won't be long before one enforcement officer would catch up with her."

"It would also make sure that it was open season on her head. There are thousands of families that would gun for her, literally!"

"Maybe. But we need to find her first."

"Right. Let's hope that people will tip us off before they tip her off the face of the earth."

Joe called the news station to put her face on every channel around the globe. "The police are calling for a worldwide manhunt for the Candlestick Massacre, Adelia. Who had poisoned and killed thousands of families associated with Loan Industries? If you see her, do not approach and make sure you contact your local police immediately!"

The Detective hung up his phone and waited for her face to hit every screen. "There is nowhere to hide."

Detective Twit turned around, suddenly noticing something move in the bush behind him. Though it wasn't an actual bush that someone had planted, it was more of an over-grown weed that had grown out from a crack in the wall. It had been allowed to grow and now resembled a shrub bush, climbing against the brickwork of a wall. The weed had grown flower heads with purple bell like shapes. Underneath the bush was a small four-legged animal. Joe knelt down to get a closer look. It was black and white with a small nose. He froze, praying that it wasn't a stunk. As he leaned closer, he breathed a sigh of relief. It was a black and white cat, curled up and was trying to keep warm from the cold. He held out a hand to stroke it. The cat opened its eyes and remained still, its ears perked up as if it was trying to hear the Detective's breath. As Joe moved forward, the cat jumped and sprinted across the road before jumping over a fence into someone's back garden.

"You scared it!" Derek laughed.

Joe shrugged. "Good, now hopefully it will find somewhere warmer than the wet pavement and a poor imitation of a bush. This is not a great place to take a nap."

"Come on, we have things to do," Derek sighed. Seeing the cat had only distracted them from their mission, and Adelia was getting too far ahead. "I really hope we find Adelia before someone else does."

Joe nodded and headed back towards the car.

They headed up the road and travel towards the Margate Village, suspecting only to end up empty-handed. The sky was already becoming dark and grim, threatening to bring a rainstorm over their heads. Undeterred, they went forward with their headlights on full.

H alf way through the countryside road, they came to a stop. It had been raining in the area. He knelt down, inspecting the sloppy mud. Embedded in the wet mud was a large tread of a tire. "Look, at last, a clue." He frowned, scratching his head. If only he knew which direction he had gone in. "Well, since he wasn't in the other direction, at least we're going the right way."

"That's great," Derek beamed. "We'll have her in no time."

Joe smiled, but the knot in his stomach hadn't shifted. "I hope so. There's a lot of deaths riding on us getting her."

Several dead ends and many grumblings later, they finally came face to face with the RV. It was parked in a car park outside an abandoned building of what used to be a high-rolling, luxurious hotel establishment.

No sooner had they gotten out of their car for the twentieth time that day, the sky opened up. Rain poured, drenching the surfaces hard and fast, drumming against the world. Lightning flashed and thunder roared above them, highlighting the edges of the RV.

Joe and Derek got closer, signalling each other to remain silent as they approached. Checking there was no one around, they pushed themselves up against the cold wet metal and peered in through the rectangular windows of the vehicle. The lights were off, and there was no sign that there was anyone inside. Joe narrowed his eyes, waiting for his sight to adjust to the darkness. After a few minutes, he could just about make out the outlines of the sofa bed, the kitchen unit, and counted three bags on the floor by the shower room.

"There's no one here," Joe whispered.

"Then why are you whispering?" Derek asked, looking confused.

"Because we're sneaking around. Seems like the right thing to do."

Derek chuckled. He couldn't argue with his logic.

Joe sighed. He couldn't very well stand around looking like he was doing wrong. "Come on. I think she might be close by. I guess she might be in the hotel. If I was sleeping on the sofa bed for weeks, I would want a bed too."

"Makes sense. Alright. Let's look. If she is in there, then we can get some backup and hopefully have her cornered."

Joe thought for a moment. There had to be a way to stop Adelia from driving away again. He looked around to see if there was anything he could use. Laying on the floor were some sticks, cigarette butts and some sharp stones. Nothing that would delay anyone unless they were walking barefoot. Even then, it wouldn't stop for very long. He sighed, thinking hard as he tapped the side of his head as though he was trying to knock something loose. Along the side of the property, he noticed a screw. He smiled. Finally, something an abandoned building had an abundance of. He searched along the edges and picked up the sharpest nail he could find. "The reason we shouldn't play in the abandoned buildings. There are a lot of sharp objects on the floor." He smiled and walked back over to the RV and placed the Nail near the tire. Then, taking off his shoe, he used the heel to hammer the nail in and watched as the tire went flat. He pulled the nail out, and did the same to the other tires, making sure that there was no way she could drive it away. He now only hoped that when he finds her, she would be alive.

Inside the hotel, the floors were bare. There were only tiny pieces of fabric nailed down on what used to be a thick red carpet. The walls were shedding its white paint, peeling and flaking from the surrounding walls. Mould had spent the empty years claiming the walls and ceiling, creeping over the surfaces like a plague.

"This place hasn't seen a cleaner in decades. What do you think happened to this place?" Derek whispered.

"I dunno. I think I remember reading something about it shutting down, but I never read into why it shut down. I just assumed that someone wanted to buy them out, so they can make the money themselves. You know, just get a bit of redecoration and get put under new management. I guess that didn't happen."

"That's a shame," Derek sighed. "It looks like it would have been nice here. I bet it made a lot of money."

Heading upstairs, it did not take long to find the high priced rooms, though they no longer look it. The doors were open, and the curtains were holy and dusty, eaten for years by moths. Joe sighed. Each room seemed more depressing than the next. The wardrobe doors were hanging off its hinges, and the windows hid in thick dust. At the end of the hall, a door that was a little different from what they had seen.

"Look there," Joe whispered, keeping his footsteps light.

"What, another door?" Derek replied, not seeing why they had stopped.

"Yes, another door. Obviously, that goes without saying. But this one is different, look."

Derek looked, straining his eyes. He frowned, trying to see what Joe had seen. It was hopeless. "I don't see what is different."

"Seriously?" Joe huffed. "It's right there. It is obvious, just look."

"I am trying. Maybe it's a slightly different colour?"

Joe groaned, "These doors are open, right?"

"Yes. I noticed that. It's like someone went round opening them all to pick a bed to sleep in."

"Yes, all the doors are open all the way or only partially. Except the one att the end. Look, it is closed."

Derek blinked. He saw it was closed. "I saw that," he frowned. "Huh. I wonder why it didn't get my attention. I completely dismissed it."

"You were looking for something hard to see. I was looking for something that was different, like a clean or closed door."

"Of course, I wish I thought of that." Derek grumbled. Sometimes he surprised himself. He can notice a lot of things, but sometimes he felt as though he had seen nothing. "How can I see everything and still be so blind?" he grumbled to himself. "It wasn't as if it was hiding."

"Cut yourself some slack. I am sure there would be plenty of times that you see something and I would likely completely miss it because I am looking for something else."

"That is true. Thank you," Derek replied, brightening up. "Lets see if she is inside that room."

They crept forward, trying not to make any noise.

They approached the door holding their breathes before joe nuzzled the door open with the tip of his shoe. The room was still, and a small flicker of a flame reflected against the back wall. A sign that someone was in there. Joe frowned. It seemed unlikely that someone would leave a candle unattended. It would bring a lot of unwanted attention in her direction, which she is trying to avoid.

As they crept through the door, Joe pushed himself up against the closest wall to his right. He shuffled his feet, feeling the way through the room to see if he can get a better view. Adelia was sitting on her bed, facing the other direction. There was no electricity, so she was reading a book. The candle was beside her, tall and slender white stick of wax. He frowned. It wasn't scented. He wondered if that too would give away her position. He shook his head, wondering why she had not thought about the glow from the candlelight would not do the same.

Derek followed him, pressing himself tightly against the wall, remaining close to his partner. "What is she doing?" he asked in hushed tones.

"She is reading a book," he muttered quietly.

Adelia paused, halfway through turning a page, her fingers still between the pages of what she had read already. Joe held his breath. Now was the time to get some backup. He sighed. She had almost heard them, so perhaps now was too late for that. He cleared his throat and called out. "Hello Adelia. We have been looking for you."

"Who's that?" she demanded.

"Detective Twit and Detective Bell," Joe called out.

"Really? That's your names? Those names sound made up to me. Are you sure you're even cops?"

"Yes, we are Detectives. Please come out peacefully. There are many people looking for you about those candles that you made. You have killed *thousands* of people lately," he growled.

"So, you're here to do what? Kill me? Hand me over to the families and let them rip me apart? Perhaps you would like to hand me to the people who tried to kill me first?"

"I know they tried to kill you. They set your house on fire and tampered with your car."

"So, what is your plan?"

Joe stepped out to face her. Derek followed closely behind, his hand ready for his gun.

"I am here to arrest you for terrorism, multiple murders and public endangerment. I would add trespassing, but let's be honest. There weren't a lot of places left to hide."

"I'm looking at a death sentence, aren't I?" she sighed.

Joe nodded, "Yes. But at least it would be relatively painless."

"And thousands died. Not millions?"

"Why would it be millions?" Derek frowned. A knot tightened in the pit of his stomach. "Please tell me there weren't more than just the three states?"

"Three states? You're kidding, right? The entire company had tried to kill me. So, in kind, I am just returning the favour. If I die, I am taking the whole damn company with me. There is nothing you can do about it." Adelia laughed, standing up as she held her hands out for the cuffs. "Yes, take me to my death chamber. I get a quick and easy death, whilst the company worldwide would die a slow and agonising death."

"Wor—worldwide?" Derek repeated. "Did you say worldwide?"

"What? Did I stutter?" she laughed. "Serves them right. If they hadn't gone and tried to kill me, they would be alive right now. But no. They wanted me dead. They get their wish, but I am taking down as many of them as I fucking can. And the best part, when the world goes to shit, I won't have to be here to see it. I can watch in hell with the rest of those assholes!"

"You're a nasty piece of work. Why didn't you just ask for protection?"

"Ask for protection? No. I am not a coward. Let them try to kill me, but I will not die without a fight."

Joe shook his head, trying to understand what she was saying. "But families are dying- including babies!"

"A small mercy for what's coming," she grinned.

"What is to come?" he demanded, really not wanting the answer to this.

She reached into her pocket and pulled out a copy of an email, confirming one hundred and seventy-eight more deliveries were sent.

"What have you done?!" Joe gasped, horrified at the implications. "What the hell have you done?!"

"I'll tell you after we get to the station," she smiled. "Where I won't be fed to the Loan Industries co-operation."

"Tell me right now," Joe growled. "Or I'll ask for a clumsy executioner instead of a decent one!"

"Alright, if you insist. But remember, you asked for it."

She took a deep breath and smiled. "I had more candles made." she stated. "And some people are going to get a very nice present. It's my way of saying thank you to the world."

"The kind that you sent to your colleagues?" Joe asked.

"No, these are much nicer. I can't wait to see how happy they look when they open it. Do you think you can get me a viewing?"

Joe swallowed hard, finding his mouth had gotten dry. He licked his lips, trying to return the moisture. "Come on," he huffed. "We better get you back."

Joe and Derek lead her to the car and headed back towards the villages. They drove through Margate, past the small stalls they had passed and past a park area with a sign to keep out. They went through the Manhattan Village and then onto the long stretch of countryside to head towards home.

When they arrived back at the station, there was a large angry crowd waiting for them. They blocked the entrance, armed with blades and torches. Joe shook his head. After the long drive, he was becoming agitated, and they were leaning on a last nerve.

"Let me through," he told them, keeping his voice to a low growl.

"Hand us the killer and be on your way," a voice shouted. Joe frowned, squinting. He was sure he recognised the voice from somewhere.

"I know that voice... either way, please move. I wouldn't want to arrest all of you for obstruction."

"Hand her over. We don't want you getting hurt. She killed our families- now she is going to die."

"She is a terrorist, of course she is going to die!" Joe laughed. "So stop what you are doing. She'll get what is coming to her, I swear it. The law is there for a reason."

"And if she doesn't get the death penalty?"

"Then she will get something that is just as harsh. I don't make the rules, I just obey and enforce them. If you carry on, then you would be in just as much trouble."

"Fine. But if she doesn't get a death that she deserves, then we will take down the law into our own hands- and do what real justice means."

"That makes little sense," Derek commented. "You got your words muddled."

"That is because I am angry! She dies a gruesome, painful death, or we'll all take the law into our own hands."

"See," Joe grumbled to Adelia. "The world has gone to shit. This is what you have done."

He looked at her face, waiting for some sort of remorse, a glimmer of sadness in her eyes. Maybe the recognition of what she had done was so wrong.

She looked back at him with a bright smile, rolled down her window, and watched. "Yes," she grinned. "And I am loving it."

Derek sighed. They were simply not getting through to her. He turned to face the suspect; the woman looking proudly at what she had accomplished. "Why have you done this? I do not understand."

"It is easy," she replied. "They moved me from building to building to get rid of me, built me up to the top of the ladder, then just as quick, made me homeless, tampered with my car, took away my job, then what home I had left was burnt to the ground. Do you really think that after being pushed and pulled and tore down, and nearly killed, was going to make me a nicer person? You're wrong. It just takes out all the kindness I had left- and I tried hard to cling to it. But after trying to kill me, they can all go to hell."

Chapter 23

They walked into the courtroom, surrounded by the angry relatives of those who had been killed. "Death sentence!" the crowd chanted. "Give her the death sentence!"

"Hanging!" they cried. "No, beheaded!" the crowd grew more angry. "What about the electric chair?!"

The judge sighed, shaking his head. "We are not barbarians," he announced. "She has already confessed to her sins. Her sentence to death was a quick decision by the jury. But she will not go like the traditionally butchered. Nor will I will grant her the grace of a quick death."

"What method will she die then?" the watchers cried out, wailing the injustice.

"She will go the same way she killed her victims. By candle light."

The crowd cheered, stomping their feet as they walked her to her cell. "We will carry her death sentence out in two weeks."

As the judge ended the trail, they watched as Adelia walked out of the room in handcuffs. The onlookers spat and kicked as she walked past them, beaming.

Joe sighed. There had to be some way of stopping the candles from being used. He frowned, thinking perhaps the news could come in handy again. He bit his lip. Adelia was aiming for worldwide panic. After giving it a lot of thought, he had the news rerun the news, with the additional update to include any candles they receive. If they don't know who gave it to them, to throw it away.

He called the news with the plan and hoped for the best. It was all he could do without causing a mass panic.

Detective Twit and Detective Derek Bell walked out of the courtroom after the barrister took the woman into custody. He took a deep breath of relief, however temporarily, now that she was off the street.

"That was frustrating," Derek grumbled. "At least she can't make any more. But now, what about the rest of the fucking world that she sent those candles to?"

"We used the news to warn people. It's all we can do."

"And what if some of them didn't see the news or had already started using the candles? We still could hear a lot of bodies piling up."

Joe sighed. He had a point, but what more could he say? "Well, I suppose we can email all the coroners around the world to monitor the symptoms. The major hospitals would already been told as soon as the news aired."

"I know, but it still bothers me. The deaths are going to keep happening for a while, and there is nothing to be done."

"We can't kill Adelia twice. What more do you think we can do?"

"I don't know. I just feel like we could do more," Derek sighed. He shook his head, snapping himself out of his funk.

"Come on. I need a coffee."

The angry mob of relatives gathered outside the courthouse, waiting to hear the verdict. Not all of them could go inside; there simply wasn't enough room.

"How is she to die?" Thomas called out.

"The same way your families did. With her own candles."

"That's irony for you," Thomas laughed.

"Hardly. The judge knew what she had done and wanted her to suffer as much as everyone else. It seems only fitting to suffer the same fate."

"When? When is she to die?"

"In two weeks. She does not have long," Derek reported.

The crowd went home cheering and singing, how her death would be remembered throughout the years.

Joe looked unsettled. His eyes became distant, as though he was looking past the surroundings.

"Do you think she had planned this?" Joe pondered worriedly.

"I don't know, maybe. It seems strange, and there was a candle in her house. Maybe she had intended on dying with the candles just the same as the others. But considering that it was such an awful way to die, it seems unlikely."

"Probably more of a ruse to throw the suspicion off herself," Derek stated, not giving it much thought.

"You're probably right."

They stepped into a Starbucks that had just opened on the corner of the road by the court. It was an ideal place to be. After a rough day or after a great day, a cup of coffee seemed fitting. A large cappuccino or Americano coffee, to celebrate a fitting end to a hard case. An espresso for when they need something stronger. It was the perfect place to be.

As they entered the shop, they scattered the tables around the room as though they had thrown in it. People were sitting down, talking among themselves in a low chatter. Joe counted three people who were drinking coffee whilst typing on their laptops.

Derek smiled, enjoying the busy chatter. An ambience noise he could listen to a lot. "I am amazed that I hadn't been in here before."

"It's new. I don't think many people had been here before," Joe chuckled. "But I agree, I love the atmosphere in here. It might be my new favourite place to go."

"Mine too. This place looks awesome. But let's not decide until we have tried their coffees."

Derek laughed. "That sounds like an excellent idea. I'm going to have a cappuccino. What are you getting?"

Joe thought for a moment, weighing out his options. "I think I will have an Americano. It's a coffee shop. If I am going to decide, it will have to be based on real coffee."

"You're the coffee drinker, if you don't like it, then chances are, it's crap!" Derek laughed.

They ordered their drinks and then went to find a seat.

The line to get coffee was becoming longer now, and the tables had filled quickly. The ambience noise had now turned into a loud chatter of noise, everyone talking all at once. Babies cried in the background, dishes and cups clattered and the sound of the coffee machine was almost drowned out by the noise of the customers. Still, they sat leaning in towards their large cups that got placed on the table in front of them. "Thank you," Joe called out, trying to be heard. The waiter nodded before hurrying off to clean the tables.

After they finished drinking their drinks, they stood up to leave. "How was it?" Derek asked.

Joe shrugged, "Honestly? It wasn't the greatest cup of coffee I had. It was a little burnt."

"Damn. Not quite the best place, then."

Joe shook his head. "I think that if it hadn't gotten so busy, this place would be fine. But as soon as it got busy, they started rushing. I think they missed a bit of ground coffee when they cleaned it out."

"Ok. Let's try it again another day when it is more quiet. Then they would have no excuses for burning your coffee," Derek chuckled. "Still, the ambience noise of quiet chatter was good whilst it lasted."

"Yes, definitely," Joe laughed. "I'll be back in the morning for another try."

Joe looked at what time it was on his watch. It was coming towards nine o'clock at night. The streets were once again black, with the dim yellow light reflecting against the wet pavements. "At least the rain had stopped."

"Thankfully. Time to go home. I'll see you tomorrow, bright and early." Derek grinned.

Joe nodded and waved his goodbye before heading to his car. He was pleased Adelia had been caught at last, but the gnawing feeling at the pit of his stomach was eating at him more than ever. Something was very wrong with this picture, but he just couldn't work out what.

"What am I missing?" he grumbled, feeling lost.

The two weeks passed with no incidents, and the news of Adelia's imminent death was everyone's conversation. Everyone gathered around the area, waiting for the flickering light of the candle.

Chapter 24

Adelia was led into her room, where she would wait to die. She smiled, politely asking for some paper and a pen. "It would be nice to have something to do whilst I am waiting for the poison to kick in."

Not seeing anything wrong with the request, they handed her a felt pen, so that she would have nothing sharp, and handed her a sheet of paper.

She walked into the room and sat on a chair, chained to a desk. The desk was nailed to the floor, ensuring that she could not escape. The candle was placed high against a shelf, away from Adelia so that it could not be blown out. Everything was as she had planned. She smiled. They could see the flickering flame through the window for miles around, and everyone would know that she was dying.

"Why are you smiling? You're about to die?" Joe demanded.

"Because you all think that you have me beat."

"We do. You're about to die. And no one is lighting the candles that you sent."

"Not everyone owns a television. The bodies will keep rising. And everyone will know my name. They will remember me as a part of history for centuries."

Joe sighed. There was something still bugging him, and he was running out of time.

The executioner lit the candle and walked out of the room. Joe and Derek followed closely behind him and slammed the metal door shut. The bolt slid along the bracket and then locked the door. There was no chance of escaping now. All they had to do was wait for the news of her death.

As the flame flickered out, the public cheered. The high-pitched cheer echoed across the streets, signalling that the woman was likely dead. The executioner, armed with a gas mask, entered the room. He leaned over her limp body, checking the pulse on her neck. Her skin was cold and clammy from her fever, her colour had paled and her pulse had stopped. He confirmed her death and walked away.

The executioner signalled for the body to be carried to the morgue. They looked at the pale, lifeless woman on the trolley.

"What did she want the paper for?" Joe asked.

The executioner handed him the folded paper with a shrug. "I don't know. It's addressed to you and Detective Bell, though."

He opened the paper and froze. He blinked, trying to make sense of the words on the page.

"This isn't over."

Joe frowned. "That makes no sense. We caught her. She's dead. The candles have stopped being produced. We have told the world not to touch the candles. What does she mean it isn't over?"

Derek shrugged, "Come on, this is Adelia we're talking about. She is just getting into your head. Don't let her get under your skin. It's done, and she is gone. The case is over."

Joe sighed. He had a point, of course. "You know what? You're probably right."

They headed back to the station and put all the case files away. Before heading out to the staff room, he paused. "I am just going to check on something."

He walked over to the autopsy room and approached the medical examiner. He cleared his throat, making himself known. "Can I ask for a favour?" he asked.

The medical examiner turned to face him, placing her hands on her hips. "What is it?"

"Something is bothering me about this. Her room was scarcely untouched. She seemed to have not thrown up, or lose her hair. Heck, not even the runs. She was just cold and clammy. Perhaps you can do an autopsy to find out why she had died with fewer symptoms than the others?"

"What do you mean?"

"I am thinking, what if she had exposed herself to the poison already? If she had introduced herself to it earlier, and poisoned herself gradually. The candle in her cell would have finished her without too much effort. She wouldn't have had so much symptoms—like a flu shot?"

"Maybe. I'll give her a check just to be sure. But I don't understand what difference it makes? Dead is dead."

"Yes. But if she had introduced the poison early on, then that means she had this all planned out. Right down to her dying. She might have something else in the pipeline after her death gets confirmed."

"You're looking too much into it. Dead is dead. Maybe she simply wanted to make sure that she died with more dignity than her victims had."

"Perhaps. That sounds plausible," Joe agreed.

"I'll check, anyway. But for now, count it as a win?" she smiled.

Joe sighed, "I will try. But there is something I am missing. I know there is. I just don't know what. Since we caught her, I have been analyzing it. Something isn't adding up."

"I am sure it will come to you," she smiled. She pulled back her long hair into a bun and pulled the body out of the draw. "Go on," she insisted. "Go home to your wife."

Derek headed home, driving slowly in his car. He was in no rush. His wife wasn't there waiting for him, there was no pet waiting for him by the front door. He sighed, feeling alone.

Joe drove towards his house and pulled up to the curb.

His wife stood by the front door to welcome him home. "How was your day? Adelia's death was all over the television- and something about those candles!"

"Oh well," he sighed. "It mentioned not to light the candles if they don't know who it was from, right?"

She nodded, "Oh yes. They were very clear on that."

"Great. I need a shower. I stink of death."

"Did you go into the room? Wouldn't you have been exposed to?" she worried.

"No, Megan. It's fine. I just stood outside the room until the woman's death was confirmed," he assured her.

She passed him a large coffee and sighed, "It is still awful business. I just hope that the news got to everyone on time. You know, the time differences and all? Some people are a whole day ahead of us, and others are half a day behind us. I worry about the ones that are ahead of time that may have already lit the candle."

"So do I," he replied.

The phone rang in the middle of the night, startling Joe from his semi-sleep.

"Hello?" he groaned.

"Hey, it's the medical examiner, Suzie?"

"Hey. What's the verdict?"

"You were right," she told him. "I have just finished doing the autopsy, and she had a lot of it already in her system. However, I do not think that she intended to do it like that. She had been exposed to it for a too long of a period. I am almost certain that she exposed herself to the poison whilst she was making the candles."

"So the quick and tidy death was a chance of luck, just because she was poisoning herself slowly?"

"Yes. I am sure that she would have thought that she would have the injection, since that is the more common method that the courts kill the convicted."

"Alright. Thank you, Suzie," he yawned. "I will see you in the morning for the final written report."

The medical examiner said goodbye and hung up the phone. Joe put the phone back on the bedside unit, glancing at the time, and went back to sleep. "Two thirty," he yawned. "Now that is dedication."

The next morning arrived with a thick layer of fog.

Joe woke up and made his way down the stairs with heavy feet. He switched on the coffee machine and switched on the television. The news was on, once again warning the public not to light the candles if they did not know who the candle was from and to use extreme caution. "On that note, the world leaders of one hundred and seventy-eight countries had received a candle this morning. Someone had left the candles on the window seals of their offices and homes, in the hope of getting lit."

Joe swallowed hard, feeling a large, dry lump in his throat. "The hundred and seventy-eight candles were to world leaders?!" he gasped. He closed his eyes, hoping that they had used their common senses and decided not to light them. A knot formed in his stomach. What if someone was not warned? What if he had missed something and an entire country suffered? Nausea washed over him like an icy cold wave of water, and he was drowning in it.

Megan joined him downstairs and stood behind him with a worried frown. She folded her arms, keeping her pink dressing gown wrapped tightly around her hoping to keep warm from the morning cold air. "What's wrong?" she asked him.

"The extra candles that were made, they were sent to the world leaders. Kings, Queens and Presidents were all sent a candle this morning. It's on the news."

"Dear heavens!" she gasped. "That's treason, right? Isn't that a death sentence as well?"

"Yeah, but the person who made the candles is already dead. We can't kill someone who has been dead for twelve hours already."

"What are you going to do?" she asked, as though she was expecting an answer.

"Uh, I really don't know. I am going to have to speak to them all and find out who put it there."

"I just had an awful thought," she gasped.

"What?"

"Well, what if there were some people who wanted the thrones to themselves and teamed up with Adelia?"

"It's a little farfetched," he smiled. "I don't think she had help all over the world."

"Well, I hardly think that she made all of those candles by herself. Think about it, thousands upon thousands of candles being made, all whilst she was on the run. It just doesn't seem likely."

Joe blinked. "Wha—What?"

He stared across the room like a light had just been switched on inside his head. He blinked again, his eyes widened. Alarm bells in his head rang like a thousand alarm bells ringing all at once. "I think you just found out what was bothering me for the last two weeks!"

"I have?" she laughed. "Oh good, I like to help when I can."

He grabbed his phone and immediately called Derek, tapping his fingers impatiently on the kitchen unit.

Megan continued to make the coffee that Joe had made, humming a merry tune to herself.

"Derek, we have a huge problem," he said, his tone was serious and boarder-lining on madness.

"What's wrong?" Derek asked, sounding almost scared.

"Something had been bothering me for the past two weeks, and I couldn't put my finger on it. Until now."

"Yes, I remember you saying something was wrong. What happened?"

"My wife helped and actually said out loud what had been bugging me."

"So, what is bothering you? Don't leave me hanging."

"The candles. All the fucking candles," he replied dramatically.

"Joe, the candles bothered everybody. It killed people."

"No, Derek. All the fucking candles. How did Adelia make and send out thousands of fucking candles whilst she was on the run? You can't run and make thousands of candles at the same time. You need a factory and stay located!"

"Are you..." he cleared his throat, sounding hoarse. "Are you suggesting that she had help?"

"Dude, I am out right stating it. The bitch had an accomplice."

"Well, dammit Joe! Who?"

Joe swallowed hard, waiting for the ground to swallow him whole. "That's just it. I don't know. And those extra candles were sent to the world leaders. Presidents, kings and queens all received a candle this morning. And I really hope that they watched the news in time and did not light those candles."

"She could have started a war..." Derek whispered in horror.

"She may have started the Apocalypse," Joe corrected him. "End of the fucking world over some bloody candles, just because people couldn't be nice to her."

"What are we going to do?!" Derek demanded, now in full panic.

"Uh, hope those leaders don't light those fucking candles for a start. That would be nice. Other than that, I wish I knew. There isn't something like this in the rule book. I am gonna have to think of something."

"I hope so," Derek sighed. "I've got nothing better to do. I'll get my stuff and come over. I'm gonna stay for the day. If we come up with something, then it would be time well spent. I hope your wife won't mind?"

"I am sure she will be fine with it," Joe agreed.

It was almost half an hour before there was a knock on the door. Joe opened it and stepped aside to let him through. "I have heard nothing yet. So maybe we have gotten lucky. Either way, we need to find out who the accomplice is."

"How? No one liked her. Who would help her kill thousands of people?"

"I am not sure. I would rather worry about the accomplice after we confirm those candles had not been lit."

"And we are going to do that how?"

Joe banged his head against the face of the wall. "I don't know. We can't go around the world to see them all. It would take too long."

Derek frowned, trying to shake his own brain for an idea. "Well, what about an email?"

"Not everyone would understand what's written."

"The news again?"

"Nah, that would cause worldwide panic. That's the last thing we need right now. Mass hysteria would bring the end of the world that much faster."

The phone rang, bringing the Detectives to a stunned silence as dread sets in. "Yes?" Joe answered.

There was a long pause as Joe's face became pale. "We'll be right there."

He hung up the phone and turned to his partner with a look of foreboding.

"What now?" Derek groaned.

Joe shrugged his head. "Shit has got bad. We've been asked to get to the station right away. An announcement is being made."

"Who from?" Derek pondered. It wasn't like there were many people that had that kind of power.

"The chief."

"Damn it. All right. Let's get going. Hopefully, we'll still have our jobs by the end."

Joe nodded. "If we survive this, I am asking for a pay rise."

"Pay rise? If we live through this, I am asking for a promotion!"

"A promotion? I hadn't even thought of that. I wonder if we can both get one?" Joe grinned.

"I hope so. Come on, they'd be lost without us holding their hands. Let's see what trouble they have gotten themselves into now."

They arrived at the station. The room was filled with their colleagues. The silence was almost deafening, listening as their footsteps echoed along the marble flooring.

"Thank you for joining us," the Chief announced.

"What's the problem?" Detective Joe Twit asked.

"The problem is that there is still a lot of mess to clean up. Unfortunately, Adelia has made a lot of people unhappy, and a lot of people dead. We need to make sure that this doesn't turn into something else."

"Turn into something else?" Joe asked. He frowned, not really understanding.

"Something else, like having it patterned and bought online by everyone else, for instance. God knows, there are many people out there, and a lot of them are killers. We do not need these people getting their hands on the equipment."

"Right..." Derek agreed.

"Good. You both have three days to find the stuff that the candles were made from. And then I want to make sure that it is destroyed."

"Destroy evidence?"

"No, of course not. I want to make sure that the equipment is brought in to the evidence locker. We have a room that doubles as a panic room. It can be put in there."

"And we have three days?" Derek checked.

"Three days."

They headed to their cars, their heads pounding.

"I am not going to survive this," Derek grumbled.

"None of us are," Joe agreed.

Derek's phone rang. He looked at the screen and groaned, seeing his ex-wife's name flash on the display. "What?" he demanded, answering the phone in a foul mood.

"That is how you're going to talk to me now?" she demanded angrily.

"You're my cheating ex-wife. How the fuck did you think I am gonna be talking to you? You're lucky I even answered the phone!"

"I don't get you. One minute, you send me a present, and then you scream at me? What the hell?!"

"What?! Has cheating on me made you delusional? Why in the world would you think that I have sent you anything other than a divorce paper? Which is on the way, by the way!"

"I got a present in the mail. The post woman had me sign for it. It had your name on it, saying that it was from you."

Derek licked his dry, cracked lips. His throat became scratchy. "Wh—What was inside the present?"

"It's a candle. It's so pretty, and my favourite colour too and smells great. But if you didn't send it to me, then who did?"

Derek closed his eyes. He really didn't want to have this conversation. "It wasn't me. Please, please tell me you hadn't used it."

"Used it? What you mean, light it?" she asked. "Of course I did. I thought it was from you."

"How much?" he demanded, his tone now becoming panicked.

"How much what?"

"How much did you use?!" he screamed.

"I don't fucking know!" she screamed back. "I've used about a quarter of it, I guess?!"

He could hear her taking a deep breath. "Is the candle still lit?" he asked in a shaky voice.

"Yeh, should I blow it out?"

"Fuck yes, blow it out!" he gasped, trying to breathe. "I am coming over to you. For heaven's sake, please use no more candles until you know for sure it was from someone you knew! Confirm first!"

"Why are you screaming at me?" she asked again, her voice became high and shrill.

"Because—Haven't you been watching the news?" he replied, exasperated.

"Of course not! It's all doom and gloom! What the hell is it gonna tell me I have not heard before?"

"I don't know," he growled, rolling his eyes. It was a good thing she didn't see it. He knew she would simply sulk and refuse to listen to reason. "Maybe something about those candles killing thousands of people and not to light them up if you get one without seeing who is giving it to you first- someone you know given you the candle!"

"Did it really?"

"Yes!" he screamed again, mostly through his own fear now. "It's—you need to get your shoes and coat on. I am taking you to the hospital for a checkup. Hopefully, you haven't used enough of the candle too much. With any luck, as long as you don't use it anymore, we can put you on bed rest until the damage is reversed..."

A few moments passed. He could hear her breathing into the microphone. "You're scaring me. Why would I need the hospital? Tell me what the hell I have missed now?"

"Argh, I am outside. Get in my car and I can explain on the way."

She pouted but did as she was told and begrudgingly climbed into the passenger side of the ford.

"Right," she said, fastening her seat belt. "What the hell have I done?"

"Basically? You're lucky to be alive. You lit a poisoned candle."

"The candle was poisoned?" she gasped. "Am I going to die? I don't want to die!"

He sighed, trying not to think of what would happen next. "Yes, I am sure you don't. Hopefully, though, only using a quarter of the candle might be harmless other than making you feel a little unwell."

"Hopefully? That doesn't sound very positive to me."

"The others used at least half right up to the whole candle. So, only using a little, you might have gotten off lightly."

"Great," she muttered. "Another fuck up. I fucked your brother, and now I have fucked myself right up, too. At least you won't have to worry about divorcing me. I would already be buried."

"I am trying not to think about that, think positive. Like it's less than half, which means less likely to kill you."

"And more likely to make me ill because I have used it?"

"No. You might be unwell, but you could simply spend a few days at the hospital to make sure that the poison is out of your system and that you're back to being healthy before they let you go."

"Right."

"Have you got the receipt?" he asked, frowning.

She handed him a small sheet of printed paper and had a close look as he took it from between her fingers.

"Hm," he hummed thoughtfully. "It looks like it was being held and then only got shipped a couple of days ago. That would mean that it got sent the day they killed Adelia."

They arrived at the hospital and went straight to the accident and emergency department. He showed the receptionist his badge and leaned in over the desk. "I need someone to look at her. She received a candle and hadn't been watching the news," he explained.

The receptionist looked at her, and then lead her into a back room for some privacy.

"Is she someone you know well?" the receptionist asked.

"Yes, she was my wife," he replied. "Please, look? She says she only used a quarter of the candle. She thought it was from me. I hope that by some amazement, maybe the damage hadn't been done yet?"

"Let's take a look," the nurse replied. He nodded and gave her half a smile.

"It's Darcy, right? We met before, when all this started."

The nurse nodded. "Yes. Unfortunately, Colleen isn't feeling too well today, so she is at home. I'll be checking on her after work tonight."

He thanked her again and went to walk around with his ex-wife, hoping for some good news.

After being told to wait outside, he paced up and down the hall, fretting. He could hear mumbled voices coming from inside the next room, though he couldn't work out what they were saying. He hoped it was good news.

Darcy walked out of the room with his ex-wife following closely behind, looking less than hopeful. Less than positive. Not something that he was looking for.

He closed his eyes for a moment and took a deep breath, not wanting to ask, but he must. He opened his eyes and looked at her, waiting for a sign that everything was going to be OK.

"How did it go? Have you avoided the symptoms? Can the damage be reversed?"

Darcy looked at him, resting a gentle hand on his arm. "She is going to be fine," she said, offering a small smile. "But she is going to need to stay here for a few weeks before we allow her to go back home. The poison might still be in the air, so it would need to be aired out properly and checked over before it can be lived in again. We also need to make sure that it is all out of her system and that her immune system is strong enough for her to survive after."

"I am so relieved," he gasped, holding in his tears. He turned to his wife, trying to keep himself together. "Next time the news is on, keep it on," he croaked. "We nearly lost you."

"You already lost me when you threw me out," she replied, but offered a small smile, anyway. "Thank you for your concern and thank you for warning me."

He gave her a brief nod and left the building. As much as he was pleased that she was going to be OK, he needed to update Detective Twit, and tell him that the candles weren't just to the leaders but others as well, disguised as presents from loved ones. He dreaded the conversation. The very idea of it made him feel sick to his stomach, and it wasn't the candles.

Chapter 25

The detectives sat in the police's cafeteria and admired their new badges. After receiving the promotion, they had very little to do. They looked through the photographs, looking for something they might have missed during the initial investigation of the candles. Any sign that might show how many people were working with Adelia, or if it was simply one person to find.

Joe sighed, knowing all too well how hard it can be to look for a single person whilst they were on the run. They could hide anywhere. They could also already be dead, but without knowing who was making the candles, they couldn't be sure. A line of inquest that he was all too familiar with.

Derek looked through the statements for any mention of Adelia, even talking to anyone else. But had so far come up empty-handed. It wasn't until that he was re-watching the security tapes from the company that something stuck out as odd. He leaned in, watching as Adelia helped someone off from the floor. There was no sound, but the person on the floor appeared to be a cleaner. They spoke briefly before parting.

He looked at the image on the screen with a frown, certain that he had never seen or come across anyone remotely close to the woman on the screen. He frowned again, tapping the glass, waiting for recognition. "Who the hell are you?"

Joe approached him from behind as he leaned in closer for a look. "What have you found?"

"That woman, look. There on the floor. Adelia picks her up from the ground. Maybe she has a friend, after all."

"We need to know who she is," Derek replied.

Joe agreed. "Yes, especially if she is friendly with Adelia. I can't believe even with her being dead, there is still so much mess to clean up."

Derek sighed, "I know. I just hope that she hadn't tried to finish what Adelia started. If she sends out new candles, disguised as presents from well-known people, there could be a whole new problem."

"At the moment, I am trying to think positive and just be thankful that maybe Adelia didn't die without a friend in the world, and that she had at least one person she could talk to."

"But then why didn't she talk her out of doing this?"

"Maybe she was already too far gone?" Derek mused. "Maybe she tried and just simply didn't get through to her."

"Or maybe she knew what she was doing and wanted to help her only friend?"

Derek looked at joe with a sad look. "That is worrying me."

"Damn it! I thought we were done with this!" he groaned. "Why did I have to keep digging?!"

"Because something wasn't sitting right with you. You did the right thing," Derek replied.

"Yeah I know," Joe groaned. "I just wish I hadn't been so good at what I do."

They went back to Loan Industries, holding the picture of the woman on the floor. Joe sighed, hoping that this time, the woman would be easy to find. "As far as she knows, she has gotten away with murder. We might get lucky."

"We don't get lucky very often," Derek agreed. "One problem, though. We don't have any proof that we have her as an accomplice. She might deny everything."

"If she does, then we'll have to be smart. I am sure she will do something stupid. Adelia isn't around to keep her in the dark anymore."

Joe grinned. "And then she will get the same fate as her friend."

Joe paced around the room, trying to think of a plan. He had done this a lot. He also found that he frowned a lot more since the case started.

They knocked on the office door and waited for Johnathan, the CEO of Loan Industries, to open the door and greet them with his fake smile. Instead, the man at the door was a security guard, wearing a scowling red angry face, with obvious displeasure at seeing them.

"What now? Adelia is dead. What do you want?"

Joe held out a picture of the woman, pausing before he spoke. "ILook at this," he said.

"It's the cleaner, so what?"

"Yes, and look at who was standing next to her. Someone liked Adelia, after all."

"You seriously can't be judging a friendship on that? They only spoke a couple of times! That's not proof of being friends—that's proof that she was there at some point whilst the floor was being cleaned."

"None-the-less, I want to know where she is," he demanded.

"I don't know where she is," Johnathan grumbled. "She hasn't been to work since that day. Gave her notice there and then, after Adelia had told her not to be walked over. She took that as a message to quit. I don't know where she is. Heck, I don't even remember her name."

Joe groaned, "And you wonder why someone tried to kill you all?"

He laughed. "Some of them tried killing her first. If they had succeeded, then we wouldn't be having this conversation at all."

Joe couldn't argue with that. He had a good point. "No, we would ask about someone else and solving Adelia's murder instead."

"Well, regardless, I am sorry, but I can not help you." Carl called out.

Joe and Derek walked out of the building, scratching their heads. "How is it that someone was everywhere, and no one remembers her name? Is anyone really that invisible?"

Derek shrugged. "I guess she didn't want to be noticed. And with these lot, I don't blame her."

They headed home, with not much more that can be done. With only a face, no name and not even in the building when the candles got made, was she even considered a suspect?

"Come on," Joe huffed. "I think we're done here."

Derek shrugged, "Yeah, I guess. I am so glad that we got her. And my ex-wife is going to be OK. Thank goodness."

The chief walked in, calling them into her office.

"Ah, Detectives. I would like to see you for a minute."

"Yes, Miss?" Joe asked.

"Well, you two really upped your game over these six weeks. How do you feel about a promotion?"

Joe blinked, looking at his partner. "A promotion? That would be awesome."

"Heck, yeah!" Derek cheered.

"What comes after Homicide Detective?" Joe frowned.

"Superintendent Twit and superintendent Bell sound good to you?" the Chief asked.

"Yes, it certainly has a nice ring to it," Joe grinned.

Derek beamed, watching as the Chief handed them a new shiny badge. "Thanks!"

"Off you go then. Be back bright and early tomorrow. I imagine that you haven't slept since this started."

"You'd imagine right," Joe laughed.

They headed out of the building and headed home, beaming.

"It's a great ending to an awful case. We deserve this!" Joe beamed.

Derek laughed. "I couldn't agree more."

Epilogue

Lilian sat at home, watching the news. The candles incident had blown over and were no longer reported on the news. They reported they had promoted the Detectives Twit and Bell to superintendent. "Curious," she mused. "They had a promotion for solving the case?"

She looked at the end of her room. Her thick purple curtains hung against the backdrop of her windows, giving her room a purple tint.

She smiled and walked up to the curtains, adjusting them slightly so that the gaps between the curtain couldn't be seen.

The newspaper articles hung on the wall in frames, each describing the candlelight deaths, and named the most heinous crime to have hit the world for centuries. She smiled proudly and faced a picture of the fireplace of her friend. "You did great," she beamed. "Everything was just as I planned." She turned around, opening the fridge, ignoring the cooling wax on the bottom shelf. "Most heinous crime in centuries? Wait until they get a load of me." She switched off the television and laughed. "Clever and remain invisible, so no one would give you a second thought."

About the Author

Michelle Mackenzie is the writer and author of the published novel, The Dark Queen series (Book 1): The Storm Within. Encouraged by the sucess of her book, she is continuing to her career as a thriller and suspense writer.

Read more at www.reflectivelinepublishing.wordpress.com.

About the Publisher

Reflective Line Publishing was launched in August of 2022. Though the company is based in the UK, the founder isn't stopping there, with plans to become a global company and become one--if not the biggest--publishing company.

If you enjoyed reading this book, and would like to keep up-to-date on new books available, subscribe to our mailing list using the link below. You can also find more information about the company on our website.

www.reflectivelinepublishing.wordpress.com

Official Mailing List

24 Bulwark Road,

Shoeburyness

Essex SS3 9RT

England, UK

Printed in Great Britain
by Amazon

84185187R00099